BRYNNDE

A REGENCY ROMANCE

M PEPPER LANGLINAIS

CHARACTERS

Bernaud Archambault, Lord Averland
Lucienne Archambault, Lady Averland
Mr. Nicolas Archambault
Miss Brynnde Archambault
Miss Contessa Archambault
Sherborne Sommerford, Earl of Darley
Georgina Sommerford, Lady Darley
Garrick Sommerford, Viscount Burbridge
Mr. Graeme Sommerford
Lady Julia Sommerford
Lady Eleanor Sommerford
Sir Everret Crabbage
Lady Martha Crabbage
Miss Violet Crabbage
Mr. Oliver Crabbage
Mr. Gerald Dallweather, a gentleman
Molly, a maid
Various Others

1

———

*B*rynnde's thoroughbred kicked up dust as she spurred him up the tree-lined carriageway. She kept her own head low under her wide-brimmed hat, more in the hopes of not being noticed than for keeping the dust from her eyes. She was in trouble and she knew it.

She rode astride the horse, having "borrowed" some of her older brother Nicolas' clothing. It was something she did often, and her family had long since ceased to prevent her, except on days like today—days when important guests were expected to arrive. Brynnde had ridden out early that morning, fully intending to be back and presentable before nuncheon, but she had managed to get herself into a long conversation with Mrs. Davershire, wife of the gamekeeper, which had led to a visit to the gardener Mr. MacDonald to check on the recovery of his broken leg, and so she had lost track of the time.

If the tenants were at all appalled at the sight of a daughter of the house riding in masculine fashion, they kept it to themselves. Surely, in Brynnde's mind, that topic of conversation around Aux Arbres and the nearby village of Barrow Wood would have worn itself out long ago.

But now they would have something new to fuel the gossip, namely Brynnde's disgraceful arrival.

She came to the front of the house and was off the horse even before they'd come to a full stop. Tossing the reins to a groom who came rushing forward, Brynnde dashed into the house and headed directly for the stairs. But she hadn't climbed more than three rungs when the familiar sound of her mother's throat clearing stopped her. Turning slowly, she saw her mother's plump but imperious figure standing in the parlour doorway.

"Brynnde," was all her mother said. It was all she needed to say.

Brynnde hung her head, the wide brim of her hat hiding her eyes.

"Take the hat off," said her mother.

Without raising her head, Brynnde reached up and pulled the hat from her long, dark, loose curls.

Lucienne Archambault, known in company as Lady Averland, glanced over her shoulder into the parlour then reached back and eased the door shut so that their guests might not hear or see what was occurring in the main hall. "Again, Brynnde. You know we've given you long leash around Aux Arbres, never demanding half of what we might, letting you run wild all over the countryside. All we ever ask is that you act with some grace, some propriety in front of company, and yet you can't even seem to manage that. Do you want to ruin your sister's chances?"

Brynnde swallowed hard, keeping hot words in the back of her throat. "No," she whispered. It was all she could trust herself to say.

"I can't hear you," her mother said.

"No, Maman."

Her mother nodded with small satisfaction. "Very well. Go on up and get yourself together. Tessa's in blue, so why don't you wear your rose?" It sounded more like a command than a suggestion.

"Always need to show Tessa to advantage," Brynnde muttered under her breath as she pushed into her room. She tossed her hat onto the bed then tossed herself after it, lying on her back to stare up at the canopy. The soft greens and cream colors of her room helped soothe her bubbling anger.

Once her breathing had returned to normal, Brynnde got up, shed her brother's filched garments and went to the washbasin to clean up. She twitched the rose tea gown from her armoire—a dress she had a personal distaste for, but then what did she care what these people saw her in?—and rang for Molly to come help her with it. Then she settled herself in front of her vanity to pull up her hair while she waited for her maid.

Molly was a sweet girl, and always quick to answer the bell, especially when she knew her mistress was already late. "Oh, this is such a nice one," Molly said when she saw which gown Brynnde had lay out.

Brynnde snorted. "It's a terrible color, and you know it. But mother insisted."

Molly didn't answer. Instead she waited patiently while Brynnde finished pinning her natural ringlets—Brynnde took pride in doing her own hair—and then helped her mistress into her dress.

BRYNNDE TOOK a deep breath at the threshold to the parlour. From inside came the continuous murmur of conversation; already the sound of it made Brynnde sleepy.

Straightening her shoulders, she stepped into the room. The talk trickled to a halt as everyone turned to regard her. Brynnde coolly returned the stares.

"Lady Darley," her mother said, rising from the settee, "may I present my other daughter? Brynnde, this is Lady Darley."

Of course Brynnde knew exactly who Lady Darley was; she'd heard of nothing but the Darleys for months. Brynnde made the pretty curtsy as she'd been instructed many times over then sought a seat on the edge of the party, across from her sister.

Contessa—Tessa for short—was summarily considered the beauty of the family and the Archambaults' best chance at a solid claim to society. Bernaud Archambault was a baron, Lord Averland, but the title was still relatively new, going only so far back as Brynnde's great-grandfather. It didn't help matters that the family came from French stock, now that the France had declared war on Britain.

Brynnde's mother was determined that the Archambaults would solidify their status by making strong matches in society. Brynnde's older brother would certainly have his choice of valuable brides—Nicolas might not rank high in society, but he was rich and also stunningly handsome, and he had any number of local young misses dangling after him, although he hadn't shown any interest yet in settling down. And Brynnde's younger sister Tessa was a beauty; she would be an Incomparable should she make it as far as a London season. But Lady Averland was hoping that expense would not be necessary if Tessa could be betrothed before then.

As for Brynnde, it had been determined that she was

unlikely to "take" in London. Not that she was sorry not to have had a Season; she would hate to be away from Aux Arbres, unable to ride the countryside and visit the tenants. Brynnde never once considered that she might not be welcome to stay at Aux Arbres once Nicolas married and started a family of his own.

Now, across from her, Tessa lifted a delicate eyebrow. Tessa was fair, her hair silvery blonde and full in its curls, her eyes the same color as the pale blue of her dress. Tessa had a small rosebud mouth and was dainty in size, while Brynnde was tall and willowy, her mouth more generous and her features stronger. But she shared the same blue eyes as her sister, brother, and father.

"I don't recall seeing you in London last Season," Lady Darley declared, breaking into Brynnde's thoughts and causing her to turn.

"Surely you cannot remember *everyone* you saw in London?" Brynnde asked.

Lady Darley reared up in her padded silk chair, and Lady Averland hastily interjected, "Brynnde was not well enough last year to endure the rigors of a Season in London."

Brynnde looked to Tessa; it was the first she'd heard that she had been ill. Across from her, Tessa's pink mouth twitched in an unbecoming smirk.

Lady Darley turned her attention back to Brynnde with renewed interest. "She's well enough now, I daresay?" she inquired, sounding for all the world as if she might be appraising a horse.

"Certainly," said Lady Averland.

"Then, Miss Archambault, will you be sharing the upcoming Season with your sister?"

Brynnde looked to her mother for an answer, and Lady Averland began, "Actually…"

"Surely the girl can answer for herself?" Lady Darley said, her eyes remaining fixed on Brynnde.

"Indeed I can," Brynnde replied. "And I won't be sharing the London Season with my sister. I have absolutely no desire to be traded off like a heifer, my money for some man's title."

If Brynnde hoped for a dramatic reaction, she was disappointed. Lady Darley only nodded. "But do you have a head on your shoulders, girl? Can you be useful?"

"I'm educated, if that is what you are asking," Brynnde said.

"More than embroidery and pretty speech and dancing?"

"I have a head for numbers, actually. Maman can tell you that I often handle the accounts at Aux Arbres."

But Lady Darley didn't bother to ask Lady Averland for confirmation; she merely took a sip of her tea.

"Where are Lady Julia and Lady Eleanor? I thought they would be arriving with you." Lady Averland remarked after an interval.

"They will be coming up with Graeme and Garrick," said Lady Darley mildly. "My hope is that they will arrive in time for dinner. It is good of you to take us a full day earlier than the other guests; I simply detest arriving at a house party with everyone else. It makes it so difficult to feel settled."

"Well, of course, we are delighted to have you stay," Lady Averland said.

The conversation went on to cover whom would be attending, a list imprinted on Brynnde's brain through constant repetition the past weeks. Brynnde tuned out the dialogue and stared out the window at the sunlight slipping over the spring hedges. The grounds of Aux Arbres were fresh and green and Brynnde wished she could be riding over them right then, far from the stuffy parlour.

Finally, Lady Darley rose from her seat in indication that tea was at an end. Lady Averland and her daughters rose as well. Brynnde looked again at Tessa, whom so far as Brynnde knew, had not spoken a word the entire time. After Lady Darley and their mother exited, Brynnde threw her arms up in a rather unladylike stretch and let loose a gaping yawn.

"She *would* arrive without Graeme or Garrick," Tessa grumped. "Now how will I catch either of them before everyone else arrives?"

"You heard Lady Darley," said Brynnde, "they should arrive tonight, and the others begin arriving tomorrow. Besides, you know Maman has planned this whole thing to showcase your charms, so there won't be any rivals to detract from you."

Tessa was clearly not persuaded as her creamy brow furrowed. "Perhaps," she conceded, though her pout remained. "I'm going up to nap before dinner; I don't want to appear tired when they arrive."

Far from tired herself, Brynnde went out to stroll about the garden that she'd been admiring from the parlour. She hadn't been out long when she spied Nicolas striding across the lawns after a day of riding the estate.

"Bryn!" he called when she waved to him. "Are our illustrious guests arrived?" he asked as she fell in step beside him to head back towards the house.

"Lady Darley is here, although I did not see the earl," Brynnde said. "The rest of the family is expected to come some time before dinner."

Nicolas grinned. "I'm sure Tess is all a-twitter."

"She was rather put out about it, actually. She's afraid she may have some competition and would like a head start."

"Competition?" Nicolas scoffed. "But Contessa is the loveliest creature on the planet! An Incomparable!"

Brynnde knew her brother did not speak with any sense of irony; it was generally accepted within the family that Tessa *was* the loveliest creature on the planet, or at the very least in England. "Don't remind her," Brynnde said. "She's insufferable enough as it is, and won't be able to do the pretty with a swelled head."

Nicolas laughed and guided Brynnde into the house, giving her a peck on her forehead. "Sounds like someone is jealous. No worries, Bryn, there will be plenty to go around. After all, Tessa can only pick one in the end."

With that, he headed up the stairs to wash for dinner.

"JEALOUS MY LEFT SHOE," Brynnde grumbled as she paced her room. Molly was on her way up with hot water for washing.

"Molly, do you think I'm jealous of my sister?" Brynnde asked when her maid entered with the water.

"You? Jealous? Of Miss Tessa?" Molly asked in huffing grunts as she lugged the water to the washstand. "What for?"

"Exactly!" Brynnde agreed, stopping her pacing and drawing herself up to stand by the fireplace. "Tessa may be pretty, but she's so addlepated! She has no real conversation outside of fashion and low-slung gossip. She barely said a word to Lady Darley this afternoon."

Molly swallowed any thoughts she may have had on the

subject as she went to the armoire to select a dinner dress for her mistress. "Did you have any idea which gown you might like to wear tonight?"

"The green one, I think," Brynnde said, moving to the washbasin.

"Oh, that one do look nice on you! As I hear it, the Darleys have *two* available young men in the family," Molly added slyly.

"And if I dare make eyes at either one of them, both Tessa and Maman will be all over me like scalded cats," Brynnde replied. "Not that I'm interested in the least."

Molly merely remarked, "They did arrive just a bit ago."

"Maybe they'll be too fatigued from their journey to join us then," mused Brynnde.

"Oh, I doubt that," said Molly. "They were a right enthusiastic bunch, chatting and laughing. I wonder you didn't hear them coming up the stairs."

"Mm," was all Brynnde said. She was done with her washing and had slipped on the gown Molly had laid out for her.

Molly came over to lace it up. "What about your hair?" she asked.

Brynnde glanced at herself in the long mirror standing in the corner of the room. "Mm," she said again, and the moment Molly was done with her laces, she took a seat at the vanity.

Brynnde did not often bother with dressing her hair, preferring to let it fall loose and despite her age and mother's antipathy, but she was quite capable of managing it without help when the occasion called for it. "Maybe my diamond pins," she said. "But no, that's far too fancy for a simple dinner. I should save something like that for the ball. Maybe just ribbons then."

Molly nodded her agreement and went to the drawer where the ribbons and trimmings were kept. She selected cream ones to match the lace trimming on Brynnde's dress. Against Brynnde's dark curls, the ribbons were bright like wedding doves.

"There," Molly said with satisfaction after tying the ribbons into Brynnde's hair. "Right pretty. Miss Tessa can't look any lovelier than you."

THEY GATHERED in the drawing room after the dinner bell rang, and Brynnde stood awkwardly by one of the bookcases, watching everyone else mingle. Both Graeme and Garrick Sommerford were tall, with fair hair. Garrick, the older son, was leaner than his more robust brother, and tanner; he had a worldlier look about him. Brynnde remembered someone having mentioned that Garrick Sommerford spent much time abroad, and when he was in England he was typically in London and almost never at the family estate of Ridgemow.

Graeme, on the other hand, seemed very warm and outgoing. He talked knowledgeably of country matters, speaking fondly of Ridgemow.

"Yes," Garrick's voice rose above the general chatter, "Graeme looks after things while I'm traveling. I fear I'll never be able to take the reins from him at this rate."

"If you'd just stay home long enough to learn the ins and outs of it," Lord Darley remarked. Although he made his tone light, Brynnde spied a hardness around his eyes as he spoke.

Garrick glanced at his father and away, his stormy slate-colored eyes finding the windows so that he gazed out at the darkening lawns while sipping his wine.

Graeme laughed, his own mood honestly light. "I'm reluctant to give it up," he said, "although I suppose at some time I'm going to have to."

Jemmings appeared at the parlour door to announce that dinner was ready, and the party moved into the dining room. Unheeding of precedence, Brynnde fell behind the others ladies found herself walking beside Garrick.

"Am I to understand that you travel a good deal?" asked Brynnde.

If he was surprised or put out by having her there, he had manners enough to hide it. "I do. I enjoy it. And I find the country unutterably dull."

"I am sorry, then, that you were coerced into coming to our house party."

"Well, it was either come along or knock around Ridgemow alone," Garrick said.

"So we are the lesser of two evils."

Garrick actually grinned at that. "Oh, Miss Archambault, I cannot imagine *you* to be the lesser of *anything*."

Brynnde was saved from responding for they had arrived at the dining room. Brynnde took her seat between her brother and Graeme Sommerford, and across from Tessa, who had the prime spot of being beside Garrick. Throughout the meal, Brynnde watched Tessa bat her eyelashes, smile and simper. It was rather like a show. Brynnde glanced across at Garrick once or twice to see his reaction, but his face was inscrutable. He seemed not to be paying attention to Tessa's prattle, giving only the most limited answers he could manage without being impolite.

Graeme showed much more favor towards Tessa's chatter. Which, Brynnde thought, was just as well considering he was clearly a much more affable character. But Tessa rode again and again at Garrick, attempting to win his approval, because of course she would want the heir.

Brynnde also noticed that Nicolas managed the dual attentions of Julia and Eleanor Sommerford quite nicely, showing fair amounts of charm to both. But knowing Nicolas, Brynnde was certain that he was mostly entertaining himself and wasn't truly romantically interested in either of the girls. She only hoped he didn't end up injuring any feelings.

"Have you had the opportunity to travel at all, Miss Archambault?" Garrick asked over the main course. Brynnde was not immediately aware that he was addressing her, and it took her a moment to respond.

"I visited France when I was younger. We have family there."

While the rest of the table shifted uncomfortably, Garrick did not bat an eyelash. "Only to France?" he inquired.

"I am afraid so. My travels have been limited. But I've been very happy here at Aux Arbres."

"To be happy in such a situation... It doesn't suggest much vivacity of mind," Garrick observed mildly.

Brynnde's mouth fell open in astonishment. Surely this man, this *guest*, son of an earl or no, hadn't just insulted her at her own table! She looked down the table to see what the others' reactions were. Both Julia's and Eleanor's heads were bent, but Brynnde could still see the bright red of their cheeks as they blushed furiously. Meanwhile, Tessa's blue eyes sparked with amusement.

Graeme cleared his throat and sallied into the void of conversation. "It seems to me, Miss Archambault, that you must enjoy the country a great deal, as I do."

Brynnde rewarded him with a smile, sparing a sharp

glance for Garrick. He smiled pleasantly in return. "Graeme is something of a dullard himself," he remarked.

Nicolas could not remain quiet now. "Are you suggesting my sister is a dullard, sir?"

"I find that hard to imagine," Garrick admitted, "but as I've hadn't enough opportunity yet to make any true acquaintance..." He shrugged.

"That's enough," Lady Darley said roundly.

"Perhaps the ladies should take their dessert in the parlour," Lady Averland suggested.

Lady Darley rose from her seat in silent acquiescence, the men scrambling to stand in her wake, and the rest of the ladies at the table followed the sweep of Lady Darley's canary-colored silk as she exited the dining room without a word.

2

————

"I apologize for my eldest son," Lady Darley said without preamble once all the women were settled into chairs and couches. A maid came in and set up the tea table, and yet another maid entered with a tray of desserts.

"I honestly cannot figure where I went wrong with him," Lady Darley continued. "He's always been outspoken—he was a bright boy, so we let him speak his mind. We probably shouldn't have allowed it; he's impossible now."

Brynnde did not miss the glance her mother threw in her direction. "You have nothing to apologize for," Lady Averland said. "Once they reach a certain age, there is simply no stopping them."

Julia and Eleanor kept their heads bent over their dessert plates, taking tiny bites of the cakes. The girls were pretty, Brynnde supposed, each with auburn hair and vividly green eyes.

Julia glanced up as she realized she was under observation. Brynnde knew she had to say something, so she inquired, "Are the two of you twins?"

Julia smiled, and quite suddenly she went from merely pretty to beautiful. "No, I am a year older than Ellie."

"Don't call me that," said Eleanor. "It's a child's name."

"We'll be having our Season this year," said Julia, ignoring her sister.

"Contessa will be having hers as well," Lady Averland interjected. "I expect we may see you at many of the same parties and routs."

Brynnde wondered idly whether they were truly of the same social caliber as the Sommerfords, or if her mother were merely aspiring or wholly delusional.

The gentlemen entered then, Nicolas and Graeme laughing together and Lords Darley and Averland murmuring in low voices about politics. Garrick took up the rear, a bemused expression on his face.

"Miss Archambault," he said, pausing before where Brynnde sat, "I do apologize for my inexcusable discourse over dinner this evening."

Brynnde favored him with a tight smile. "Certainly, sir."

Garrick smiled as if she'd just told some famous joke and moved on. Brynnde had to stop herself from scowling after him. He was laughing at her! The apology could not have been sincere; Lord Darley must have insisted, or perhaps Nicolas and Graeme had shamed Garrick into it.

"Shall we play cards?" Lady Averland offered.

Nicolas and Graeme eagerly agreed to play against their mothers. Julia and Eleanor asked Tessa and Brynnde if they would like to make up a game. Brynnde glanced longingly out the window, where the garden lay in cool lavender twilight. Often after dinner she would stroll the garden for the last fresh air of the day, but with such a house party she suspected her usual peace would be interminably interrupted.

"I was actually hoping Miss Archambault would be so kind as to show me this place where she's spent so much happy time," Garrick said, offering Brynnde his arm. "Perhaps once I've seen it, I'll better understand what holds her here."

Brynnde looked up his arm into the blue-gray eyes, prepared to refuse in case he was prolonging the joke at her expense. But Garrick's tan skin set his fair hair blazing, and Brynnde found herself distracted, wondering what he must look like in sunlight. Aware she was staring, and that he was beginning to smile again, she pushed the thought aside and responded, "There's very little to see at this time of evening; the lawns will soon be dark."

"Then we'd best make haste," Garrick said.

Brynnde didn't miss Tessa's dark look as she accepted the proffered arm. "You might all come," she suggested suddenly. It seemed only fair, considering the girls could not make up a game of cards without a fourth, and it was unlikely that either Lord Darley or Lord Averland would be very interested in playing. In any case, she could hardly go walking in the dark with a man without a chaperone.

The other girls eagerly agreed and Tessa didn't hesitate to take Garrick's other arm. As they exited the house, Brynnde removed herself to walk behind with Julia and Eleanor. The group promenaded along the paths lined with nodding flowers, though it would be a few weeks yet before the gardens were in full bloom. That was Brynnde's favorite time of year, when all the flowers burst into color and their comingled fragrance hung heavy in the evening air.

She would have preferred to walk alone with her own thoughts but knew she could not neglect their guests. Truly, Brynnde supposed she should be grateful to Garrick for giving her the excuse to enjoy her customary stroll. She asked his sisters, "Do you travel a good deal as well?"

Eleanor kept her wide eyes fixed on Garrick's back as Tessa's laugh tinkled out over the still evening air. Julia was the one to answer. She said, "Not as much as Garrick, certainly, but we do spend a part of each year in London."

"I like Ridgemow better," Eleanor said. "I'd rather not have a Season and just stay home."

"And marry Thomas Dryer," Julia teased.

"Be quiet, Julia," said Eleanor.

"Is there a chance Mr. Dryer will be in London for the Season?" Brynnde asked.

"Not in the least," Julia said. "He's not…"

"Not what?" Brynnde pressed.

"Not of our ilk," Julia finished.

"Oh, just say it," Eleanor sighed. "Thomas Dryer isn't gentry."

"He's a merchant," Julia explained.

"The son of a merchant," Eleanor elaborated. "And due to take over his father's business before long."

"But can't you get him to London somehow?" Brynnde asked. "Merchants must go to London all the time." She wasn't sure that was true, but it sounded reasonable.

The sisters looked aghast. "To what purpose?" asked Julia.

But Eleanor's eyes were twinkling. "That would be perfect!"

"No it wouldn't!" said Julia. "Eleanor, even if Thomas were to come to London, Mother would never relent. You'd never be allowed to marry him!"

They ambled a bit farther, trailing Garrick and Tessa down toward the low wall at the far end of the formal garden. Brynnde thought the two looked quite a matched pair with their fair hair, though Tessa was of course much paler and her eyes more blue than the stormy, almost gray shade of Garrick's. Tessa was short, too. Next to Garrick Sommerford, she looked a mere child.

As if reading her thoughts, Eleanor asked, "Does your sister have designs to marry our brother?"

Brynnde looked ahead to where Tessa clutched Garrick's sleeve tightly enough to make her knuckles white. Tessa was looking up at him through her lashes, her doll-like face framed by her fair curls. Garrick looked down at her and smiled as he spoke. Tessa giggled girlishly in response.

"We don't often have the fun of guests," Brynnde hedged. "It's so nice to have people visiting, instead of having the same old discussions over dinner."

"She'd get sick of Garrick's stories soon enough," Julia predicted.

"If she got *that* far," Eleanor added. "Garrick is hardly the romantic. She'd be better off working on Graeme."

Brynnde's hand flew to her mouth; she wasn't sure whether to laugh or be offended. A low chuckle floated on the night air—Garrick's amusement at something Tessa had said.

"He may not be full of romantic notions," Brynnde agreed, "he doesn't strike me as such. However, your bother does seem to like adventure. Which, if played right, could lead to a romantic end for you, Lady Eleanor."

"Oh, do just call us by our first names, at least when it's only us," Julia said. "No need to 'Lady' everything up."

"Indeed, then you should call me Brynnde. Or Bryn, for short."

"What a singular name! Is it French?"

"I don't believe so," said Brynnde. "In fact, I'm not at all certain where my mother discovered it." In fact, Brynnde knew exactly how she'd been given her name, but it was not a story she was inclined to share.

"In what way do you believe our brother can enable my romance?" Eleanor asked.

"We could possibly pose it to him as an entertaining scheme to get your Mr. Thomas Dryer to London for the Season. If your brother could arrange for Mr. Dryer to attend some of the parties, you might be much thrown together."

"And perhaps our parents could then begin to see him as respectable," Eleanor deduced.

"He comes from the working class, to be sure," Brynnde said, her mind whirring; she loved having a reason to use her problem-solving skills. "But if he has a solid head for management and a decent income, and more importantly, if you truly are in love..."

"Oh, we are!" Eleanor exclaimed.

Julia rolled her eyes. "At every country dance, Thomas never fails to stand up with her. Twice."

"You're just jealous!" said Eleanor.

The words brought back to Brynnde an earlier conversation, and she flicked a glance at the couple strolling ahead of her. But Garrick and Tessa had stopped walking and stood waiting for their companions beside the garden wall.

"I thought I detected a bit of strife," Garrick said amiably once the ladies had approached.

"Just vivid conversation," Brynnde replied.

Garrick lifted his eyebrows. "I was telling your sister that you have a lovely garden. I much prefer it to the one we keep at Ridgemow."

"You prefer anything to Ridgemow," Eleanor muttered.

Garrick turned sharply to her, but clearly thought better of saying whatever had come to his lips.

"It's a wonder you could see anything of the garden to enjoy it," Brynnde said. "It's beginning to be solid dark. We should probably go back to the house."

"Would they lock us out?" Garrick asked.

"They almost never lock the doors," Tessa assured, and Brynnde could tell she wanted to linger.

Garrick glanced at Tess as if surprised to find her still at his side. "We should probably go in now in any case," he said. "I would hate for any of you lovely flowers to catch a chill."

While they'd been standing and talking, Garrick had disengaged his arm from Tessa's grasp. Now he took Brynnde's so that they could begin making their way back to the house. "Only fair," he said, "that I accompany one sister down and the other back."

Eleanor plucked Brynnde's sleeve as they began to walk, and when Brynnde turned to look she saw hope in the younger girl's face. Brynnde nodded in understanding and worked to pull Garrick a few steps farther up the path. She wasn't sure why, but she didn't want Tessa getting wind of their scheme.

"Lord..." she began then realized she did not know how to address him.

Garrick's lips twisted at her discomfiture. "Your mother did not require you to memorize all our titles? No, really, it's refreshing," he added as Brynnde's mouth fell open. "My father is Lord Darley, as I will be, and for now I'm borrowing his second title as Viscount Burbridge."

Had Maman mentioned that one? Probably, but Brynnde had a habit of tuning those things out. "Lord Burbridge," she said slowly as if testing its weight with her tongue, "will you be in London at all for the Season?"

Now Garrick eyed her with suspicion, and Brynnde

fancied the night had suddenly grown a tad colder. "Perhaps for part of it," he answered tightly. "I normally wouldn't be, but mother has requested that I attend at least some of my sisters' come out. She believes it will lend a bit of shine to them and attract a good set. And I suspect that she's also hoping I might be caught and settle down."

"You don't usually find London entertaining?"

"It doesn't hold my interest for long," said Garrick. "I much prefer to be abroad."

"But perhaps there is a way to make London more entertaining," Brynnde suggested lightly.

Garrick's frown deepened, and Brynnde felt the muscles of his arm tense. "Really? And what would that be?"

"Are you aware of your sister Eleanor's *tendre* for a Mr. Thomas Dryer?"

Garrick appeared startled then barked a laugh. His arm relaxed. "The merchant's son? I know him, but I hadn't realized she had formed an attachment. Well, she is young; she'll get over it."

"Why should she?" Brynnde countered hotly. "Just because he's from a working family? If he's kind and intelligent—"

"She's not in the market for a dog. She needs a husband," said Garrick.

"A woman seeks the same qualities in both," Brynnde said.

Garrick let out another loud laugh at that. "You really are something, Miss Archambault. Are you quite certain you and your sister bloom from the same root?"

Brynnde scowled. "You insult me yet again, sir."

"Not at all. At least, it wasn't intended that way. Please, do go on with your suggested diversion in London."

"Assuming you could be persuaded to set aside your dislike for Mr. Dryer—"

"I never said I disliked him," Garrick interjected.

"Then can you be persuaded to even contemplate the possibility of a match between him and your sister?" Brynnde asked.

"Once Eleanor gets to London she's sure to find out that she has miscalculated the depth of her feeling for Mr. Dryer," said Garrick.

Brynnde felt her feminine spirit rear in protest. "To say so is to discredit your sister by suggesting she is flighty and would easily transfer her affection from one man to another. Do you not believe she can know her own heart and mind?"

Garrick's brows went up. "I only meant that she is young yet and has not made the acquaintance of many men. But I believe you were trying to convince me that this would somehow be entertaining?"

Brynnde explained how finding ways to introduce Mr. Dryer to society would at the very least make the time go by faster. "Do you think that you might find a way to bring Mr. Dryer to London for the Season?"

"Even if I could draft some way to do it, I trust he would only have his heart broken in the end. Eleanor is likely to find love with some more eligible man during her Season. After all, right now she has not looked much outside Ridgemow. Once she broadens her horizons—"

"Oh, again!" Brynnde cried in exasperation. "In your mind no one is truly happy unless she's gone abroad and seen the world! Even if one thinks oneself happy, you are quick to assure them otherwise. And no wonder, for how could anyone be happy with you about pointing out all the ways they are wrong?" And with that she sailed ahead, speeding towards the house.

Garrick paused and turned to the astounded young ladies who had been strolling behind them. "It seems tonight is not my night to say the correct things to win Miss Archambault over," he said.

"Not *that* Miss Archambault," Tessa agreed, stepping up to regain Garrick's arm. "Indeed, she is considered rather impossible by the whole of the family."

"Then she and I have that much in common, for my family thinks the same of me. Is it not true Julia? Eleanor?"

His sisters came to walk on either side of Garrick and Tessa, Eleanor's expression sober for she could only surmise from Brynnde's sudden departure that Garrick had not agreed to their scheme. Julia's own countenance was studiously blank, as was its habit to be when she was thinking hard about something.

"There is one in every family, I suppose," Julia said at length, having given it serious consideration. "Although one might think the two of you would get on better, having sympathies for one another's place in familial regard."

Garrick laughed, even as Tessa's brow furrowed; Julia's language was too embellished for her understanding.

"One might think!" Garrick agreed. "Well, perhaps tomorrow I'll find my tongue better suited to winning her friendship."

"In the meantime, you seem to have at least one of the Misses Archambault on your side," Eleanor pointed out flatly.

Garrick looked down at Tessa and for a second time within the space of an hour appeared surprised to find her there. "Of course," he said absently. "Come on, then. It's late now, and we'll make a fine sound trooping up the stairs."

3

———

The next morning brought a steady stream of house party guests. Some were arriving from town, just for the day, to participate in the archery and lawn bowling. The Crabbage family, however, was arriving from their estate in Cheshire and would be staying the week.

The Crabbages were as dour as their name suggested, but being old friends of Lady Averland's family, she'd felt compelled to invite them. She'd been surprised, however, when their acceptance came in the post; the Crabbages were not known to attend parties and fetes; even their attendance at country dances was sparing. Sir Everret Crabbage was something of a miser—wealthy but strangely afraid of losing his money, he almost never spent any, and his house and family had been known to suffer for it. Their carriage arrived in sad condition, its paint flaking and its springs groaning in protest for want of care.

The Crabbages had two children, a daughter of Brynde's age named Violet and a thirteen-year-old son named Oliver. Sir Everret was a scholarly sort of man, as was his daughter, much given to indoor life and books. His wife and son were far more active, however, their very presence exuding restlessness that, because of Sir Everret's monetary strictures, had little outlet outside of gossip on the part of Lady Crabbage and pranks on the part of Oliver.

With the Crabbages and the Darleys installed at Aux Arbres, the house was busier than Brynnde could ever remember it being in all her nineteen years. Sitting at her open bedroom window, which faced out over the back lawns of the house and the garden they had strolled in the evening before, she could hear the commotion from the front drive as it moved into the house in a series of orders shouted over other voices and greetings and introductions. Sighing, Brynnde knew her cherished peaceful days of riding over the estate were temporarily over. She would never be able to get away with hiding or disappearing, and certainly she would not be able to steal any of Nicolas' clothes to ride in.

Luckily, though, most attention would be on Tessa. The goal of this party was for Tess to get a head start before her London season. If anyone were to ask for Brynnde that would only be a sweetener—so long as it did not end up interfering with plans for Tessa's brilliant future.

Molly arrived even as the footsteps of the newest house-guests fell away down the many corridors as they were led to their rooms to unpack and rest before the day's activities. "Aren't you coming down to breakfast, Miss?" Molly asked as she eased the door shut behind her.

"Thank you, Molly, but no. Too many people to face so early in the morning. You know I'm no good at conversation this early in the day."

"I'll bring a tray up then and give your excuses."

"Don't worry about it; I'm not hungry. But do send up some water, would you?"

Molly didn't trust Brynnde's fastidious cleaning, feeling

sure that so many washings would only make her mistress ill. But it wasn't a fight Molly was capable of winning; she'd tried enough times. "Yes'm," was all she said as she slipped back out of the room.

Sighing once more, Brynnde got up from her window seat and went to her armoire to choose a suitable morning gown. She opted for spring green muslin sprigged in yellow, hoping the bright colors would heighten her own spirits or at least make her look more cheerful than she felt.

To her surprise but also her relief, Brynnde found the parlour empty. Taking up some embroidery, she went to sit by the window and work on her needlepoint. Her technique was in dire need of practice; she'd shown no aptitude for the ladylike arts—sewing and other needlework, painting, singing, not even flower arranging. Brynnde had no eye for color except to know when she liked what she saw and when she didn't. She was an accomplished dancer, however; she had a natural grace that was the only thing in which she felt she excelled over her sister, aside from her general intellect.

Brynnde was unsure how long she was in the parlour before the Lady Darley, Lady Crabbage, and her mother came sailing in. Brynnde thought that they looked like a clutch of spring flowers, her mother in soft cornflower blue, Lady Darley in jonquil yellow, and Lady Crabbage in a pale pink that did not suit her decidedly round frame.

"Oh," Lady Averland said, drawing up short upon entering the room. There was no need for introductions, for Brynnde had known Lady Crabbage since girlhood.

"Brynnde!" Lady Crabbage crowed upon seeing the

reason for Lady Averland's sudden stop. "Oh, but I should more properly call you Miss Archambault, shouldn't I?"

Brynnde rose to meet the guests and found herself enveloped in Lady Crabbage's meaty arms. "Hello, Lady Crabbage," she said, although her words were muffled.

"I've known her since she was a child, you see," Lady Crabbage said to Lady Darley. "She and my own Violet are of an age, and they've spent many happy springs and summers together."

"Actually, it's been a long time since we've seen one another," Brynnde remarked as she removed herself from Lady Crabbage's embrace. "How is Violet?"

"Well! Well! You should go up and see her. Oh, but she'll be down in a minute anyway, I'm sure."

"And Oliver?" Brynnde went on, feeling the stress of social small talk even as her smile froze on her face.

All the ladies took seats. "Doing so well!" Lady Crabbage said. "Quite the scholar. Gets it from my side, you know."

Brynnde only just kept herself from rolling her eyes. Anyone who truly knew Oliver was aware he was far from scholarly, and that any wits he had inherited must come from his father. Oliver had managed to fool his parents for years by scraping by with average marks and not getting into too much trouble. But all Brynnde managed was, "I'm so pleased to hear it."

That was all Lady Crabbage needed to get her going on a steady stream of *on dits*, discussing their estate of Lowlea and all who lived on and around it. She threw in a few choice bits of gossip from friends in London as well. Brynnde kept her eyes mostly on her embroidery—she had to, considering how terrible she was at it—but glanced up now and again to notice that Lady Darley appeared far from invested in the chatter. In fact, she seemed to be staring rather blandly at the far corner of the room.

"Martha," Lady Averland suddenly inquired, and Brynnde suspected her mother had also noticed Lady Darley's glazed look, "are you launching Violet again this year?"

Brynnde had to muffle a groan. Poor shy and retiring Violet—her mother had dragged her to London the year before last but she hadn't "taken." Last year it had been decided that maybe it would be best to wait before trying again. After all, a London season was costly, and Brynnde suspected Sir Everret was in no hurry to spend more money. In the meantime, Violet confessed in her few letters to Brynnde that she had been subjected to any number of tutelages on poise and conversation, anything that might make her seem more vivid than she actually was. Violet *was* like her father in the very ways Oliver was not; she was scholarly and quiet, liked to read and attend lectures. She took very little care in her appearance, often appearing disheveled and frequently absent-minded.

"Yes, we will be in London for the season," Lady Crabbage said now. "Violet has quite come out of her shell, you know, and she's very excited about the whole thing. You remember two years ago, the girl was practically terrified. But she's just proven to be a late bloomer, and now she can hardly wait to get to London."

Brynnde made a mental note to ask Violet directly about that; she couldn't imagine Violet being at all excited about going to London, unless there were a lecture series going to be there at the time.

"And you, Brynnde dear?" Lady Crabbage asked. "You'll be attending some parties with your sister, I daresay. Might catch yourself a one as well."

Brynnde looked up from her needlework and forced a non-committal smile.

"Well, Lady Darley has two girls at once to launch," Lady Averland pointed out. "That will be some work!"

Having heard her name, Lady Darley snapped to. She picked up the thread of conversation without difficulty. "We've been planning it for some time now, so I don't anticipate too many problems. Unless, of course, they both fall for the same beau!"

"Oh, that seems unlikely," Brynnde said without thought, then almost gasped at how stupid she was. "I mean," she added hastily, "I had the pleasure of conversing with them both at length yesterday evening, and it doesn't seem to me they'd be interested in the same sort of man..." Brynnde trailed; she was only getting in deeper.

But whereas Lady Averland was scowling as fiercely as she dared while still managing to look ladylike in front of her guests, Lady Darley's lips were actually curled into something like a smile. "It's good of you to notice, Miss Archambault. Julia and Eleanor often get mistaken for twins because they look so much alike, and so many also assume they must be alike in every other way as well."

Even as she was speaking, a parade of young ladies entered the parlour, Tessa at their head and walking like a queen. Julia and Eleanor Sommerford followed, and Violet Crabbage came in last, and being the oldest and tallest looked somehow even more out of place than she might usually. Brynnde smiled broadly at her dear friend and slid over a little on the sofa so that Violet could join her. Together, Brynnde figured, they could feel like grown-ups.

Tessa flounced down in a chair beside her mother, looking as imperious and severe as ever. When Julia asked if anyone were doing archery that afternoon, Tessa gave a delicate shudder. "Certainly not!"

Julia threw her an odd look but refused to cater to Tessa's sense of drama by asking why, which led to Tessa's pouting the rest of the morning.

"I'll be going," Brynnde said. She did not excel in the feminine arts, but she was fair at archery and not too terrible at lawn bowling. While she'd rather be riding, Brynnde would gladly accept any excuse to get out and enjoy the weather. Besides, she found it far more palatable to engage in activities with the guests than sit around a parlour all day trying to think of things to say.

"Oh! Then I'd like to shoot too, if you don't mind," said Julia.

"Of course. Eleanor? Violet?" Brynnde asked.

Violet flushed at being singled out in a room full of people. "I'm afraid I haven't the skill," she admitted. She plucked nervously at the skirt of her gown.

"Neither do I," said Eleanor kindly. "But I'm willing to try, or at least keep the company. Perhaps you and I could practice together, Miss Crabbage?"

Violet blushed even more deeply, this time with gratitude.

"I'll practice too," Tessa announced suddenly. "After all, it would do me some good to get some air."

It would do you some good to lay aside your airs, Brynnde thought, only to be rewarded for her distraction with a prick of her own needle.

AFTER A MORNING of sore fingers from haphazard embroidery and an enforced rest after luncheon, Brynnde finally found herself free to seek the sun and air of the lawn. Her mother had instructed the servants to bring out tables and set out tea, and Brynnde sailed by where Ladies Averland and Crabbage sat conversing, snatching a biscuit on her way to the archery targets. She fancied she heard her mother's gasp, that intake of breath ready to rebuke her for her cheekiness, but the words turned into, "Lady Darley! Please do have a seat!" Brynnde breathed a prayer of thanks, sent up on a sigh of relief.

She was the first lady to arrive at the lawn but discovered the men had already started. Her brother and Graeme Sommerford were laughingly arguing over a shot one of them had made, and Brynnde reflected they had grown friendly quickly.

As if reading her thoughts, a voice at Brynnde's ear said, "They seem to be fast friends."

Brynnde turned to find Garrick Sommerford—Lord Burbridge, she reminded herself, though the name did not suit him, was far too stuffy—at her shoulder. She frowned, not liking having been snuck up on, nor having her thoughts so openly spoken by someone else. "It would seem so," she agreed.

Garrick raised his eyebrows. "You disapprove?"

"Not at all," said Brynnde. "As a rule, my brother shows good judgement in his choice of friends. If he were laughing with *you*, I might wonder, but as it stands..." She gave a tiny shrug.

Garrick placed a hand over his heart. "You wound me, Miss Archambault. Are you still angry about yesterday evening? What if I were to swear I almost never suffer such verbal clumsiness? That it must be your stunning beauty that has caused me to trip over my own tongue?"

Brynnde looked hard at him, the angelic halo of his sunlit hair, the twinkle in his slate-colored eyes. He was laughing at her! Again! "Insufferable," she muttered and stepped away to find a free target. She had a sudden and acute need to shoot something.

But Garrick (Brynnde decided it could do no harm to call him that in her head) refused to be shaken off so easily. He walked beside her as she marched up the line of archery targets until she stopped at the far end. "May I join you?" he asked as Brynnde snatched up the waiting bow.

"I'm sure I would be poor sport for you," said Brynnde.

"On the contrary, you've been a very good sport thus far."

You mean you enjoy making sport of me, Brynnde thought but didn't say. She let an arrow fly. It hit just northeast of the bull's eye.

Garrick took up a second bow. From down the line, his brother Graeme called, "Having to show off against the women, Garrick? Can't match the men, eh?" But his broad grin belied any harshness in his words; Graeme exuded fraternal affection.

Garrick returned the smile. "Actually, Graeme, she's a sight better than you. I daresay Miss Archambault here could show us all up."

All at once Brynnde discovered herself to be the center of unwanted attention. Though the townsmen would not be so bold as to challenge Brynnde, Garrick and Graeme were of high enough rank that—with Nicolas' encouragement— they were willing to play against her. The others left their targets to come watch.

Brynnde flashed her brother a glare, but he only laughed. When Graeme asked Nicolas if he intended to shoot against his sister, he shook his head ruefully. "I know better."

A young man from the Barrow Wood tavern ran to

remove Brynnde's earlier hit from the target. "You should move that fast when bringing our ale!" a fellow called to him, only to be greeted with a mix of cheers and hissing reminders there was a lady present.

Brynnde looked around. There were at least a dozen men, and she knew them all, some from town, some from Aux Arbres and its grounds. She had nothing to prove to any of them; they'd seen her ride out in her brother's clothes, and most had known her from childhood. There was no one here to impress.

Her eyes slipped over Garrick Sommerford. No, no one to impress.

He smiled again in that infuriating way. "Ladies first."

Brynnde lifted her bow. Nocked an arrow. Let fly without thinking too hard.

The hit was better than her first shot, but not by much. The arrow landed just at the edge of the red. Still, it was enough to gain admiring oohs from the gathering.

"You see what I mean," Garrick said to his brother.

"Indeed," Graeme agreed, "quite a fine strike."

"She is a veritable Diana," Garrick persisted. "It would take an Apollo to best her."

"Well, I can't claim to be that," said Graeme. "But I'll give it, as we say, a shot."

Graeme took longer, Brynnde noted, to nock and aim than she had. Then again, she reasoned, he did have something to prove, didn't he? That he could shoot at least as well as a woman.

His arrow hit lower and to the right of Brynnde's, a shave off the red, but close enough not to be embarrassing. Whistles sounded and several hands clapped Graeme on the back and shoulder.

"Apollo it is," Brynnde said, and Graeme smiled, his cheeks suffusing with pink.

"Not quite evenly matched," he admitted.

"But nearly," Brynnde said. She meant to be magnanimous, but the light that came into Graeme Sommerford's eyes at her words made her stomach flutter. Why was he looking at her like that?

Garrick cleared his throat. "I do believe I also promised to try my hand."

For once, Brynnde was glad for his intrusion; it gave her an excuse to break away from Graeme's gaze. Once she did, she felt able to breathe again.

Her smile for Garrick was genuine, one of gratitude, but when he saw it, his brow furrowed slightly. "Yes, well..." Seemingly blindly, he took up a bow and arrow, nocked, aimed, and—

"What is this crowd about?" Tessa's ringing voice asked.

Garrick's arrow went wide, and he bit back an oath.

The group of men parted and Tessa marched through. Behind her came Julia, openly marveling, and Eleanor and Violet, each ducking their heads, though Violet was so tall that she hunched by habit.

Tessa stopped at the center and shot her sister a calculating look so swift Brynnde was sure no one else caught it. Almost immediately the sweet expression was on Tessa's features as she looked up from under her lashes at Garrick. "Oh, I would love to see you shoot, Lord Burbridge," she said. "I'm sure you must be so skilled."

"I'm afraid you just missed it," said Garrick, setting down the bow. "And so did I."

A ripple of laughter moved through the group and it began to break apart, some men returning to their own targets, others venturing up the lawns in search of refreshment. The ladies, however, remained where they stood, as did Garrick, Graeme, and Nicolas.

"It's only fair you try again," Brynnde told Garrick. Her eyes slid toward Tessa. "I'm sure my sister would agree and is very sorry she intruded."

Tessa's mouth dropped open, her polite mask not merely slipping but flying off entirely. "Brynnde! How was I supposed to know—?" Then she became intensely aware of all shocked faces, the eyes trained on her. Collecting herself, the sweetness returned to Tessa's face, her eyes flying up to Garrick's raised brows. "That is to say, I couldn't see a thing with all those people standing around! I had no way of knowing you were about to shoot, my lord. But of course I do apologize and would very much like to see you make another attempt."

"Hm," said Garrick, and his gaze moved to Brynnde, his mouth twisting as if they shared a secret, though Brynnde couldn't imagine what it might be. "Well, if the ladies insist..."

"Oh, we do! Don't we?" Tessa looked around for encouragement.

Julia shrugged. "We see him do it all the time."

"When he's home," Eleanor added. "So not that often."

Violet only pulled her shoulders up as if she wished she were a turtle with a shell to crawl into.

"Such ringing endorsements," sighed Garrick. But he retrieved the bow all the same. "Let's make it interesting, shall we?"

Nicolas' brows came in. "A wager? In front of the ladies?"

Garrick smiled over his shoulder at the gaggle of misses then pegged Brynnde with his iron-colored gaze. "I was thinking more *with* one of the ladies."

Brynnde knew she should not. In fact, a proper lady

would all but faint at such a proposition. But as Nicolas opened his mouth to decline on her behalf, Brynnde said, "What kind of wager, my lord?"

Tessa gasped audibly. Violet whimpered. Julia and Eleanor were silent, but Nicolas flashed Brynnde a warning look.

"Nothing outrageous," said Garrick, as if wagering with a woman wasn't scandalous enough. "If I hit the bull's eye, you promise me the first dance at the ball Saturday evening."

Now Tessa made a choking noise. If Violet got any lower, her head would be inside her dress.

"I'm sure you could sign her dance card," said Nicolas.

Garrick kept his eyes on Brynnde. "I worry it will be full before I can claim one. And I do prefer to be first."

"Then she will gladly save you the first dance," Nicolas persisted. "Won't you, Bryn?"

Brynnde looked into her brother's worried face and her determination withered. Much as she hated to back down, she could not put Nicolas in such a position. "Of course," she agreed, "there is no need to gamble. I am honored to give Lord Burbridge the first dance. But I would still enjoy seeing him shoot." It was the most diplomatic answer she could manage, allowing both men to save face and treading the line of propriety.

The twist of Garrick's lips suggested he understood Brynnde's predicament. He did not push the issue. "Very well," he said, then glanced back at Tessa. "If everyone could just remain quiet for a moment." Again he lifted the bow, nocked the arrow, and aimed. Brynnde found herself oddly mesmerized by the fluidity of his movements; he was swift and sure in them, practiced. Under his coat, the muscles of his arms rippled like her horse Parnassus' legs—effortless power.

Brynnde was so caught up in her thoughts she hardly realized the arrow had flown until the *thwump* of its strike reached her. Unlike when she and Graeme had shot, no applause or congratulatory murmur came. Everyone remained silent and still.

The arrow stood in the dead center of the target.

4

Though Friday evening brought a spring shower, Saturday dawned bright and clear over Aux Arbres. Brynnde slipped from her bed and inhaled the quiet. The house had been a hubbub all week, so many comings and goings, though they'd seen little enough of the men outside of dinner. It was the constant gabbling chatter that made Brynnde think she might go insane, the need to be always mindful of what she said and to whom. She did enjoy reacquainting herself with sweet Violet, and she'd come to like the Sommerford sisters, but Tessa's presence put a damper on things. Not that Brynnde minded being pushed to the edge of anyone's attention, but to not be able to go out and get away from it—to have to sit in the parlour and participate—was suffocating her.

But this was the last of it. There would be the ball that night, and the next day their houseguests would leave. And if the Sommerfords left without one of them offering for her sister, Tessa would be impossible to live with. Maman, too, probably.

Brynnde's feelings on the matter were mixed. She

certainly would not mind having Julia and Eleanor for sisters. Graeme also seemed amiable enough, though Brynnde had difficulty picturing him with Tessa. And if not Graeme, it would be Garrick. That was even harder to imagine, though Brynnde could not say why except that it made her chest feel sore every time she thought about it.

Ah, well, if Tessa married Lord Burbridge, maybe he would take her abroad and Brynnde would never have to see them.

She couldn't decide if that made her feel better or worse.

Brynnde went to the window and gazed longingly out at the damp green grass. One ride wouldn't hurt, she decided. Parnassus needed the exercise and so did she. And it was early enough she wouldn't be missed. She could be out and back by breakfast, and even then she would likely be first as everyone else seemed to have adopted Ton hours, staying up to play cards and then sleeping until late in the morning.

Brynnde rang for Molly and was already half in her hunter green riding habit by the time the maid appeared to help her with the rest. Molly stifled a yawn, and Brynnde said sincerely, "I am sorry, Molly, if I woke you."

"They do have us up at all hours," said Molly through another yawn. "I won't be half sorry to have it be just the family again." She placed the matching felt hat on Brynnde's dark curls. "None of Master Nicolas' clothes for you today, eh?"

"This is as much as I dare," Brynnde said. "Having to sneak out of my own house just to go for a ride..." She disliked riding sidesaddle but would make the best of it.

The stable boy was as bleary-eyed as Molly had been, and Brynnde waved him off. "It's all right, John, I'll get him." She marched down to Parnassus' stall only to have the horse turn his head away when she tried to pat him.

"I know," Brynnde told him. "And I'm sorry. If I'd had any say in the matter, I'd have spent much more time with you."

"I'm glad to hear it."

Brynnde whirled and discovered Garrick leaning in the stable doorway. His riding breeches were the same tan as his skin, making him appear almost— Brynnde squelched the thought as her cheeks heated. She hoped she could pass it off as irritation rather than embarrassment.

"Lord Burbridge," she said, pleased with how steady her voice sounded. "Were you planning to ride?"

"Oh, no, it's just I've run out of clean clothes. These were all that was left for me to wear."

Brynnde's mouth fell open, guppied before snapping shut again. "You're funning me."

He grinned and gave a nod. "I am." Without visible effort, Garrick leveraged himself to standing. "He's beautiful."

"What? Oh," Brynnde had forgotten Parnassus despite the horse's nudging; he'd detected the peace offering of sugar she'd slipped into her pocket. "Yes, thank you."

She watched warily as Garrick strolled over. He put out his hand and the horse turned to sniff it. "Parnassus, isn't it? We have only the barest acquaintance. I haven't been able to convince the stable lads to allow me." His thunderstorm eyes glinted at Brynnde. "They say he's yours."

"He is," Brynnde said roundly. She fished the sugar from her pocket and held it out for Parnassus, thus winning him back to her. "But all the horses at Aux Arbres are magnificent," she told Garrick.

"I know. I've been out every morning." He looked down the line of stalls. "I think it's Narcissus' turn."

Brynnde watched him walk to the horse's stall and lead

out the beautiful blue roan. Garrick behaved as if he owned the place—

The thought gave Brynnde pause, and her throat closed. Maybe he expected to own the place? Well, not exactly, of course; Aux Arbres would go to Nicolas. But if Garrick were considering a match with Tessa, he would certainly make himself at home at Aux Arbres.

Finished with the sugar, Parnassus nudged impatiently at Brynnde's arm, bringing her thoughts back to the moment. She led him out and tacked him, swearing under her breath at her skirt and wishing she'd stolen her brother's clothes after all, never mind what the guests thought.

By the time she finished, Garrick had already taken Narcissus out and, Brynnde assumed, begun his ride. So she stopped short when she found him standing and waiting outside the stable, reins in hand. "I thought you might need help mounting," he explained.

Brynnde only just prevented herself from rolling her eyes and saying, "Hardly." Instead she managed a polite, "No, thank you. I'm used to doing it on my own."

Still, Garrick waited while she climbed the block and settled herself on Parnassus' back. Only then did he also mount. "Where to?" he asked.

Brynnde blinked at him. She wanted desperately to remind him he had not asked to accompany her on her ride, nor had she offered, but of course that would be rude. And if Garrick really did plan to become part of the family... Brynnde's heart hammered, but she counted it as due to irritation at having the ride she'd so looked forward to overtaken by this... this... *lord.*

Garrick apparently understood Brynnde's unspoken feelings. He said, "I only hoped you could show me more of what you love about Aux Arbres. I've enjoyed my rides here, but I'm sure you could tell me so much more about the land. If you prefer to ride alone, however, I will not impose."

Parnassus stamped an impatient hoof, and Brynnde absent-mindedly patted his neck. "I would be happy to show you the estate, Lord Burbridge. I hope you do not mind if we stop to speak with some of the tenants?"

"I'd be delighted," said Garrick, and to his credit he looked it.

By the end of the morning, Brynnde could not guess why she hadn't wanted Garrick with her to begin with. He seemed honestly interested, enthusiastic even, to learn about Aux Arbres and meet its residents. Again Brynnde wondered whether the interest stemmed from plans to unite the families. Brynnde imagined Tessa in the throes of wedding planning; she would be more insufferable than usual. Suddenly the morning felt less warm.

As they returned to the stables, Garrick said, "As to your, uh, suggestion regarding London..."

It took Brynnde a moment to understand. "You mean your sister and Mr. Dryer?"

"I am fairly certain I can get him to town."

Brynnde all but bounced on Parnassus' back. "She will be delighted!" Brynnde had grown fond of the Sommerford sisters, and Eleanor often spoke of Thomas Dryer; Cupid's arrow had sunk deep.

Garrick looked askance at Brynnde. "You will be in town, too, Miss Archambault?"

"Yes," Brynnde sighed. "I cannot avoid it. All of us except Papa are to go. He will come later if..." Her voice trailed.

"If you make a match," Garrick concluded. Seeing the look on Brynnde's face, he added, "Why are you looking at me as if I'm speaking Farsi?"

"I don't know what that is," Brynnde admitted, "but then

I also don't know why you would say such a thing. This is Tessa's Season, not mine." A blush crept up her cheeks. "I apologize. I did not mean to be so frank with you."

"On the contrary, I like that you're frank with me," said Garrick. "In any case, if you are to be in London during the season, you will almost certainly find a suitor, possibly several." His lips were puckered as if he tasted lemon.

Brynnde shrugged. "Well, I am not seeking one."

"You may not look for a stone, but a field still has many."

"Then I will try not to trip over any and hope to save my ankles," said Brynnde.

Garrick gave a satisfied nod. "Good. As you still owe me a dance this evening."

A couple of stable lads ran into the yard to take the horses. Brynnde gave Parnassus over somewhat reluctantly, patting him and promising it wouldn't be so long before their next ride.

She and Garrick walked back to the house together. Showing him around had taken longer than Brynnde had anticipated, and by the time Brynnde had cleaned up and changed clothes breakfast was well under way, though Lords Darley, Crabbage, and Averland were absent, as were their wives.

Garrick, also freshly dressed, went to the sideboard and piled his plate with toast, eggs, beans, and sausage. Brynnde did likewise, earning a lifted brow as she caught Garrick's eye.

"It's a fine estate," Garrick declared, taking a seat.

Nicolas pinked with pleasure. "I'm glad you think so." The men entered into a discussion of crop rotation and Brynnde focused on her meal, too hungry to start up a conversation with her peers.

Slowly, she became aware of hot eyes burning into her.

She turned to see Tessa's pursed rosebud mouth, her blue eyes flashing in a way that signaled temper tantrum. Meanwhile, two sets of green eyes were also fixed on her, more kindly but speculatively as well. Only Violet seemed not to be staring, her brown eyes downcast, though that was hardly unusual for Violet; she never made eye contact if she could help it.

Brynnde swallowed a mouthful of toast and started to say something innocuous, but Tessa abruptly pushed back from the table and stood. With startled glances, the men rose as well, but Tessa did not appear to notice, instead flouncing out of the room without a word.

"I apologize for my sister," Nicolas said as he and his companions resumed their seats. "She must have just remembered something."

Brynnde grimaced. She knew Nicolas was trying to cast Tessa in the best possible light, but her sister sometimes made it nearly impossible. In many cases the best light for Tess would be utter darkness.

"Are you looking forward to the ball tonight, Miss Archambault?" Julia's question, and use of her family name, brought Brynnde back to herself. Though they had taken to using one another's first names when alone, with the gentlemen present they felt constrained by propriety.

"Oh. Yes," answered Brynnde. She tried to smile. In truth, she had forgotten the ball entirely, despite Garrick's earlier reminder that she had promised him a dance.

"I'm not," admitted Eleanor.

"It's nothing against your family or anything," Julia hastened to add, though Brynnde would hardly have taken it that way in any case. "It's just that—"

"Mr. Dryer won't be here?" Brynnde guessed, and Eleanor's cheeks reddened.

"You'll still have to dance, you know," Julia told her sister. "Just to be polite."

"I know," Eleanor sighed, then added sharply, "but don't try to tell me I may meet someone I like more! I won't."

Julia shook her head and rolled her eyes.

"I'm not much for dancing either," Violet said quietly. "I've often hoped to devise a way of twisting my foot so as to have an excuse not to."

"How extraordinary!" said Julia. "I love to dance. What about you, Miss Archambault?"

"I do enjoy it," Brynnde said, "so long as I have a decent partner. There is nothing more tiring than a man who steps all over you."

A corner of Julia's mouth lifted, revealing a dimple. "Both my brothers are fine dancers," she declared. "Though Garrick is the better of them."

Garrick turned at the sound of his name. "Gossiping, Julia?"

She turned her dimple in his direction. "Wouldn't you love to know?" And with that she pushed away from the table, as did the other ladies, leaving the men to scramble to their feet as well. Though by the time they had sorted themselves, the ladies were gone.

5

---

*A*fter a morning of idle chatter and an afternoon of enforced rest, the time for the ball finally arrived. Any number of friends and neighbors were expected to attend, and Lady Averland had impressed upon Tessa that this was her last chance to attach one of the Sommerfords before having to fight for them—and others—in London.

Tessa was in a dither over the new gown that had been made for her. It was white, as all young ladies were expected to wear, and cut to accentuate Tessa's particularly lovely arms. Lord and Lady Averland had made a gift of a pearl necklace and earbobs to Tessa, who also had her maid string pearls through her upswept curls.

Brynnde had also had a new gown made for her, although less attention had been paid to her appearance. Her gown was simply and plainly made of pale blue satin with white lace for trim. Brynnde did not find it to be a particularly becoming dress, refusing to see the way the color emphasized the luster of her hair and eyes.

Molly had made rosettes of scraps of the satin and fixed them in Brynnde's dark masses. Then she brought out Brynnde's jewel box so that her mistress could select appropriate accessories. "It's a shame you haven't any blue gems," Molly said. "They would go so well with your new gown."

"It doesn't matter what I wear, Molly," said Brynnde. "It's important that Tessa catch eyes tonight."

"She hasn't been so very successful so far, so I've heard."

Brynnde paused in picking up and putting down various pieces of jewelry. "Where have you heard that?"

Molly shrugged. "Just downstairs. All the help has been watching the goings on."

"Hmm," Brynnde said, going back to choosing accessories. "What makes them think Tessa isn't doing well?" She wondered what the servants had seen or heard that she had not.

Molly raised her brows but didn't answer right away. "Well, she do have some competition."

"Who? Violet?" asked Brynnde. So far as she could tell, neither Sommerford had shown any interest in her friend. "Tessa will have much more competition in London, so if she can't pull this out now, she'd best set herself up to be fully charming during the season. What do you think of these?" Brynnde held up silver filigree earbobs.

"They do look nice with blue," said Molly, although she privately thought they were not near nice enough for such an occasion. There hadn't been many balls at Aux Arbres, and certainly none of this caliber. Even the Christmas ball didn't do this one justice.

A tap on the door sounded just then, and Molly went to answer. "Oh, my Lord!" she said, stepping back with a deep curtsey and allowing him in.

Brynnde rose from her vanity. "Papa? Is something wrong?"

But Lord Averland was smiling. "I hope not," he said,

giving Brynnde a kiss on her forehead. "I know you're not... Well, you know, not like Tessa when it comes to gowns and hair and the lot, but..." He held out a long, thin box covered in deep blue velvet. "Well, I just thought maybe..."

Brynnde opened the box. Nested in the satin lining were an aquamarine pendant and matching earbobs. "Papa!"

"I had the dressmaker show me a swatch of fabric from your gown and thought these might make a good match," he said.

Brynnde threw her arms around her father's neck. "Oh, Papa, they're lovely!"

"Well then," he said, patting her shoulder and easing himself away from her, "I'll let you finish getting ready."

After he was gone, Brynnde rounded on Molly, her lips twisted in a grin. "Blue indeed! You knew!" she accused.

"Not at all, Miss!" Molly protested. "But do leave it to Lord Averland to have good taste in the matter."

Brynnde couldn't argue with that assessment; her father had presented her mother with any number of fine jewels. He always seemed to know just what was required to complete a toilette, and Brynnde had heard her mother more than once ask her father his opinion in matching clothing, jewels, hats, scarves, shoes and the like. Brynnde giggled to think of it: her father, the fashionmonger.

"There now," Molly said, fastening the pendant around Brynnde's neck. It hung from a silver chain and had eight diamonds placed around its oval cut. The earbobs, too, were oval aquamarines that dangled from intricate silver filigree and had a diamond for each post. "Quite the right shade of blue they are, too."

Brynnde had to agree; the gemstones matched the satin of her gown perfectly.

"You'll outshine everyone tonight," Molly predicted.

But Brynnde shook her head. "No, it's Tessa's night for shining."

"In white?" asked Molly in disbelief. "Why that little miss will only manage to look washed out! She's so fair already. And here you are, looking like a jewel yourself. Who wouldn't rather look at you?"

"Molly! You shouldn't speak that way. This is important for Tessa; it means a lot to her."

"Sorry, Miss," Molly mumbled, then added more boldly, "but it might could be just as important for you, too. After all, Miss Contessa can only choose one."

"And I'll choose *none*," Brynnde said with a laugh as Molly handed over her slippers. "At least not until I have to."

"You can't live at home forever," remarked Molly.

Brynnde laughed again. "Are you so eager to leave Aux Arbres?"

"No, Miss, but I knows the way of things," said Molly soberly.

Brynnde stood and smoothed her gown, checking the mirror that all was in place. "Let's just get through tonight, shall we? There's time yet for the future."

BRYNNDE CAME down the stairs a bit earlier than the guests and joined her family in the parlour. Upon seeing her sister, Tessa demanded, "Where did you get that necklace?"

Brynnde's eyes flew to her father, who replied robustly, "It was a gift from me, just as the pearls were to you. A man has a right to give all his daughters gifts, after all."

Tessa's lips twitched in displeasure, but she did not say more. Brynnde suspected that her sister felt her night had been made less special in some way. Tessa could not stand not to be the center of attention.

"I think both my sisters look splendid," said Nicolas.

"And now we should prepare to meet our guests," Lady Averland announced. Together the family moved into the main hall to form a receiving line. Brynnde found herself between Nicolas and Tessa, feeling uneasy as ever in such social situations. But as soon as the guests began to arrive, she relaxed and was able to honestly greet them with genuine smiles. Years of riding the estate and village had acquainted her with just about everyone, and so she had no problem finding things to converse about.

Nicolas, too, was at ease Brynnde noticed. Of course he would be, since as future lord of the estate he had long been familiar with the residents.

But Tessa's charms were forced at best. Brynnde knew her well enough to know the smile was strained and the laugh hollow. She only hoped no one else could tell.

The turnout was the best they'd ever had at a house party; better even that the annual Christmas fête. Brynnde expected word had made the rounds that the Earl of Darley would be attending. For many in Barrow Wood, this might be their one and only chance of ever seeing an earl.

Once the majority of guests had arrived, the Archambaults joined them in the ballroom, which had been created by opening up two partitions to make a long room lined with potted plants and flowers brought in from the gardens that very afternoon. The room blazed with candles and the warmth engendered even stronger scents from the flowers, so that with the blooms and the perfumes and colognes of the guests, the ballroom was almost cloying in its closeness. Upon arrival, Brynnde went directly to one of the tall windows to breathe in some fresh air.

At the far end of the room was a low dais where musicians tuned their instruments in preparation for the first quadrille. Brynnde glanced down at the dance card dangling from her wrist. Brynnde had penciled "Lord Burbridge" on the first line, and many young men had filled remaining spaces in the receiving line, though the card was not entirely full. She was just checking to see when she might first have a break when a familiar voice asked, "And did you save me a waltz, too?"

Brynnde's eyes flew up to find Garrick bowing over her, hand out in expectation. She ignored it and looked again at her card. "I do have one waltz left," she said. "The Honourable Mr. Sommerford has taken the other."

Garrick straightened. "My brother?"

His tone surprised Brynnde. "Yes, why? Should I fear for my feet? You surely wouldn't call him one of those, what was it? Stones in the field?"

"Ah, so you *are* looking for a suitor," said Garrick.

"No," Brynnde told him, exasperated, "only dance partners."

Tuned to their satisfaction, the musicians struck a chord. Garrick held out his hand once more. "That much I can provide."

This time Brynnde took the hand and allowed him to lead her out. Garrick proved to be as good a dancer as his sisters had promised, and soon Brynnde's only thoughts were for the steps, the fun and flow and grace of them. She smiled openly and genuinely, her cheeks becomingly flushed with exertion and enjoyment.

Garrick, for his part, showed visible reluctance to relinquish Brynnde to the next man. He hovered past introductions until Brynnde began to frown and Mr. Dallweather positively scowl. Finally he took their meaning. "Do put me in for that waltz," he reminded Brynnde before bowing and departing.

"He means to dance with you twice?" Mr. Dallweather inquired as he took Brynnde out to the line.

"It would seem so," said Brynnde.

The figures of the dance did not allow for much more conversation, for which Brynnde was thankful. Mr. Dallweather was a very nice man but mostly given to talk about his dogs, of which he had several. He was almost as old as Brynnde's father and, as Brynnde understood it, had been married once yet briefly; Mrs. Dallweather had passed away some two years later. This always predisposed Brynnde to be kind to him, as she would want others to be kind to her father if he were to be widowed. And yet she was surprised when Mr. Dallweather informed her he would very much like a second dance too, if she had any available. She did and dutifully marked Mr. Dallweather down for it before he handed her over to Graeme Sommerford for the first waltz.

"Would you like some punch, Miss Archambault?" Graeme asked solicitously. "You appear quite out of breath."

Brynnde smiled up at him gratefully. "It's true," she admitted. "I've never been so in demand."

"I can scarce believe that." He handed her a cup of punch. Brynnde gulped it as quickly as she dared; the waltz was beginning.

The rest of the evening blurred by. Graeme's second dance was the supper dance, and so she went in with him to dine. Her brother and a young miss named Amelia Robish joined them, but later Brynnde was unable to recall what they ate or spoke about.

After supper Brynnde had a break in the stream of dance partners, and she took advantage of it by stepping outside for some air. The spring night was cool and slightly damp; it smelled of grass and dark earth. Brynnde inhaled it deeply and wished once again she could go for a walk, alone and away from the pressing heat of the party.

She was checking her dance card to see if perhaps she had enough time for a short stroll in the garden when Mr. Dallweather appeared. "Miss Archambault," he said, taking her hand rather abruptly, and Brynnde only just managed to keep from snatching it back. She didn't want to hurt the poor old gentleman's feelings after all.

"Is it time for our dance?" she asked, unable now to check her card.

"I'm hoping we have a lifetime of dances ahead of us," said Mr. Dallweather. "Miss Archambault—"

"There you are!" a voice sounded from behind the columns at the far end of the house. Brynnde turned just in time to see Garrick Sommerford step out of the shadows. "Miss Archambault, I believe this is our dance."

Bewildered, Brynnde started to say it was not, that he'd asked for the waltz, but Garrick went on, "But you do look fatigued. Let's get you inside, out of the chill, and put some punch in you, shall we? Dallweather," he added with a nod at the older man. Mr. Dallweather gave a stiff nod in return.

"That wasn't very nice of you," said Brynnde as Garrick ushered her inside. "Stealing Mr. Dallweather's dance. I thought you wanted the waltz."

"I did and I do," said Garrick amiably. "I also wanted to save you both the embarrassment of him declaring himself to you."

Brynnde gasped audibly. "That's ridiculous!"

"That he planned to propose? Or that I wanted to stop him?"

"Both! Either!" Brynnde shook her head as if to clear it, curls and earbobs flashing in the candlelight.

"Unless, of course, you would welcome his suit," Garrick said. "In which case, I am very sorry to have intruded."

Brynnde looked up at him and found his expression startlingly severe. "He's almost of an age with Papa," she said.

"Many young ladies marry older men. Some even welcome the relative security of such a match," Garrick pointed out.

Brynnde shook her head again and accepted the punch Garrick offered. "Do you know Mr. Dallweather well?" he went on.

"Well, yes," Brynnde said. "I've known him all my life, more or less. He thinks of me more like a daughter than a— a— There's simply no reason to think he would expect to marry me, or for me to marry him!" Brynnde finished.

"Then perhaps I mistook the situation," Garrick relented. As Brynnde set her empty cup aside, he offered her his arm. "But in truth, you do look as if you could use some fresh air."

"Which is what I was getting when you flew in to save me," said Brynnde. "What were you doing outside?"

"The same thing you were, save having an old man propose to me." When Brynnde raised her brows at him, he added, "Wishing I could go away somewhere." He guided her smoothly back outside.

"You are mistaken again," said Brynnde. "I do not wish to go away anywhere. I only wish to be able to enjoy my home in peace. You, on the other hand, seem only to want to escape... Wherever you are at the time."

To Brynnde's surprise, and somewhat also to her irritation, Garrick threw back his head and laughed. "You may be right," he told her. "I get bored being in any one place for very long."

Brynnde pulled her arm free of his hold. "Then I am sorry you've been forced to bear Aux Arbres for an entire week."

"No one forces me to do anything," Garrick assured her. "If I hadn't been enjoying myself, I would have found a reason to leave."

"Am I supposed to thank you for finding us amusing?" Brynnde asked archly.

"I should thank you, I think, for being so entertaining. And now I do believe that *is* the waltz." He offered Brynnde his arm once more, and reluctantly she took it.

"I must say, Miss Archambault, that I've never more looked forward to spending time in London as I do this coming season." And with that, Garrick Sommerford, Viscount Burbridge swept her into the dance.

6

"Mr. Dallweather came to see me this morning."

Brynnde froze where she stood in her father's study. As soon as the Crabbages' carriage had been lost to view, the Sommerfords having set out earlier still, she'd gone for a long ride on Parnassus, only to be summoned to her father the moment she'd returned. She hadn't even gone to change and so stood in her brother's breeches and oversized shirt under her coat.

Bernaud Archambault surveyed his eldest daughter. "Do you have any feeling for Gerald Dallweather?"

"He's—he's very kind," Brynnde said, then admitted, "talks a lot about dogs."

Her father laughed. "Yes, he does, rather." The he sobered. "You know, Brynnde, that you cannot stay at Aux Arbres forever."

His words struck Brynnde like a lightning bolt. "But I... I..."

"Marrying someone like Gerald would allow you to remain close to your family," her father continued. "He has a comfortable estate. No title, but he would be good to you, I think?"

"I don't want to marry Mr. Dallweather!" Brynnde burst. "He's very kind to offer, and I am sorry if it hurts him, but I cannot think of him as a husband." His whole house probably smelled of dogs, she thought.

Her father nodded. "Yes, well, I did not answer for you. But Brynnde, you must start to think of whom you *can* consider a husband. I know this Season in London has been bent around Tessa, but you cannot rely on either of your siblings allowing you to—to live with them indefinitely. You'll have a home here for as long as *I* am here..." He left the rest unsaid, but his meaning was clear. He wanted to see her settled, by which he meant married.

"It is my fault," her father said. "I allowed you to carry on because you are such a light to me. Aux Arbres could not be the same without you. However," and the sternness in his tone seemed more for himself than Brynnde, "it will have to be, some day. You must light another man's life. And while your mother is determined on Tessa, I am hopeful you will find someone in London as well."

Brynnde thought of Garrick Sommerford, his talk of suitors and stones. And how he'd been right about Mr. Dallweather's proposal. She pictured Garrick's self-satisfied smile and wished she could throw one of those stones at him.

"I will put Mr. Dallweather off for now," her father continued, breaking into Brynnde's imaginings. "But if during the Season you do not find someone who better suits you..." Again he let his meaning hang in the air between them.

"Yes, Papa," Brynnde managed. Without waiting for dismissal, she whirled out of the study and up to her room to change and contemplate her options. She could never, *would* never, beg Tessa for a place in her household. Nicolas, however, might be beseeched. She needn't live in the house; she'd be happy in one of the tenant cottages. A small allowance... Watching her nieces and nephews grow up... Until at last she became the family spinster everyone pitied. Tessa married to a duke or some such and constantly condescending to her. The thought of it made Brynnde grind her teeth, and she pulled her boots off rather too roughly.

But no more could she marry Mr. Dallweather! Any affection she felt for him was filial at most. She might just as well marry an uncle. The idea made Brynnde shudder.

Molly bustled in, humming. "I did hear you was back from your ride."

"That's not all you heard, I'm sure," said Brynnde.

"Well, no," Molly admitted as she collected Brynnde's— or Nicolas' rather—discarded clothing. "It's just Jemmings said Mr. Dallweather came to call, and..."

"And?" Brynnde prompted.

"Is it true you're to marry him?"

"No," answered Brynnde with a flat finality that startled even her. "Though he did ask." Brynnde marched to her wardrobe to find something fresh to wear.

"Your father turned him down?" Molly asked breathlessly. Brynnde knew this gossip would make her maid much sought after below stairs. Gossip worked the same everywhere; those privy to it were rich in immaterial ways.

No matter. Brynnde had always been forthcoming with Molly. "*I* turned him down. Or, really, I told Papa I didn't want to marry Mr. Dallweather."

Molly nodded her approval as she began fastening the back of Brynnde's orchid-colored gown. "Too right. He's far too old for you. And his house probably smells of dog."

Brynnde laughed aloud at Molly having pinned her exact thought. Then she inhaled deeply. "Papa says I will have to marry Mr. Dallweather if I don't find anyone else."

"Well then," Molly said resolutely, "the sooner we get you to London the better."

Brynnde had seldom been to the house in Berkeley Square; she had no reason to go, nor any desire to either. Tessa, on the other hand, often begged for trips to London, and was at the height of bliss at finally being there. Even as they walked through the door to the townhouse, Tessa was listing all the shops they would need to visit in order to complete her wardrobe.

Brynnde found her room and hid for as long as she could until Molly's unpacking drove her out again. Not in London an hour and already Brynnde yearned for a quiet corner somewhere. There would be no escaping the bustle, the noise. Weeks of comings and goings stretched ahead of her, relentless, unless Tessa managed to secure an offer first thing.

Oh! But if she did, Brynnde would have no opportunity to find a suitor of her own! So she could not even hope for a quick end to the Season. She was well and truly stuck.

Brynnde ensconced herself in the library, a room she was certain neither Maman nor Tessa would enter. Nicolas might, but him Brynnde could tolerate. She stayed there in peace until forced to go change for dinner.

The meal was mostly Maman and Tessa chattering about where to go, and who to see, and which parties they'd already been invited to, and to which they should inveigle invitations. Nicolas made good-natured suggestions only to be scoffed at and told he clearly did not know... Whatever it was there was to know. Brynnde's mind wandered until she heard the name Sommerford spoken.

"They're coming this week," Maman said, "and I do expect to renew our acquaintance." She looked fondly at her youngest child. "They took quite a shine to you, didn't they, Tessa dear?"

Over the handful of weeks since the house party at Aux Arbres, Maman and Tessa had reworked history to suit their desires. The initial petulance at a lack of interest from either Garrick or Graeme had become a story of how the two brothers were locked in a fight for Tessa's hand. London, they were sure, would produce a winner.

Brynnde, meanwhile, wondered whether Garrick had succeeded in getting Thomas Dryer to town. After all Eleanor's glowing words of undying affection, Brynnde was keen to meet the unparalleled Mr. Dryer herself.

"But clothes first, dear," Maman reminded. "We cannot go out in our country frocks. Certainly not!" She looked at Brynnde for the first time. "Papa says you are to have new clothes, too, Brynnde. He's right, of course. Can't have you looking like a poor relation."

Which is how Brynnde came to find herself standing in the midst of a dressmaker's shop, surrounded by more fabrics and furbelows than she'd ever dreamed existed. The options extended far beyond those of Mrs. Caverley back home. And while Tessa more or less ordered one of everything, Brynnde attempted to keep her requests simple. "Maybe one like this," she said, pointing to a pattern that had nice lines that Brynnde felt were ruined layers of lace and ruffles, "but without so much... stuff and nonsense on it?"

"Oui, Mademoiselle," the dressmaker said, though Brynnde suspected she'd somehow offended the woman.

After buying what felt like half the shop, they took fabric samples to the milliner to order matching bonnets. Then it was on to shoes. Brynnde felt sure she would need new ones after just the one day of walking all over Bond Street.

Finally, they returned to the carriage. Tessa complained of having to wait for her new fripperies, but Maman told her it was better to see it done well than quickly.

"But what shall I wear until then?" Tessa wailed.

Maman patted Tessa's hand. "We'll make do. Our first party isn't for another week yet, and Madame Odille promised to have at least a couple gowns ready by then."

"I shall be ashamed to even go out in public," Tessa insisted.

Brynnde could take no more. "You *are* in public," she pointed out. "And in a perfectly nice gown that Mrs. Caverley worked hard to make for you." It was a gorgeous butter yellow that set off Tessa's golden curls, and her bonnet had a ribbon to match.

Tessa scowled, crossed her arms, and turned resolutely toward the window. Then she spun back around to look at their mother. "A week! All the best gentlemen will be engaged already!"

Brynnde stifled a laugh. Tessa's faith in society's efficiency knew no bounds. Everyone would pair off like animals going to the Ark. How orderly!

Then Brynnde sighed. If only it were so simple.

Two days later, Brynnde found herself set upon by her sister and mother as she sat in the library. She'd picked up a novel to read, and while it was not quite as good as going for a walk or a ride, Brynnde was sucked into the story of a young woman staying in a very strange house filled with shadows and unidentified noises. When the library door flew open, Brynnde jumped a mile where she sat.

"Brynnde, they're here!" Tessa squealed without preamble. Maman came after her, saying, "Tessa, do be still! Your hair, you mustn't—"

"Who is here?" Brynnde asked.

"The Sommerfords!" Tessa cried.

Brynnde was on her feet before realizing it. "All of them?"

"Just the ladies," Maman reported. "But it is enough that they wish to maintain our connection."

"Of course they do!" snapped Tessa. She tossed her curls, sending Maman into another dither. "But the men can't come to call themselves," Tessa reasoned, "so they have to send their mother and sisters. They probably want to know what other suitors I have."

Brynnde smoothed down her skirt and ran a hand over her own hair. "Yes, I'm sure that's it," she said dryly. In fact, Brynnde's heart was leaping at the idea of seeing Julia and Eleanor; she hoped they would be able to talk quietly enough that she might learn whether Mr. Dryer was in town.

"It's funny of you to take such an interest," Julia remarked once she, Eleanor, and Brynnde were whispering together in a corner of the drawing room. Brynnde's mother and sister kept casting glances at them, but Lady Darley looked upon the threesome with such a fond eye that Lady Averland dare not say anything against it.

"I'm sorry," Brynnde said, immediately chastised. "It is, of course, none of my concern."

"Oh, but it was your wonderful idea!" said Eleanor. "And only you could have convinced Garrick to help. If I'd asked, he'd have given me a lecture and that would be the end of it."

"You have seen him?" Brynnde asked, her embarrassment forgotten.

"We just happened to cross paths with him on our morning walk," said Julia. "Which reminds me, we wanted to invite you to come out with us tomorrow afternoon."

"Then you'll be able to see Thomas—Mr. Dryer—for yourself!" Eleanor said.

Brynnde took in Eleanor's glowing cheeks and sparkling eyes and couldn't help but smile. "I would love to. I am sure Maman won't mind." She glanced over her shoulder at her glowering mother and hoped it was true.

Lady Darley once again became the saving grace. As she stood to leave, she directly invited Brynnde and Tessa out on the morrow. "We'll be taking out the barouche," she said, and with a thoughtful eye added, "You girls are thin, you should all fit."

Just before slipping away, Julia leaned in to Brynnde. "She's only inviting Tessa because she has to." Then with a beaming smile and in a flurry of auburn curls and lacy dress hems, they were gone.

7

Tessa darted in and out of her room, shouting to her maid, in yet another uproar over having nothing good enough to wear to Hyde Park. Brynnde and Molly merely exchanged glances in the looking glass as Molly finished buttoning Brynnde's robin's egg blue dress. Then she waited for Brynnde to put up her hair before handing over the matching bonnet. Brynnde sniffed at the flimsy thing. "It will hardly protect my face from the sun."

"Maybe not, but it do look nice on you all the same," said Molly as she tweaked a bow into place.

Brynnde hated bonnets, and was not fond of hats in general, no matter how nice they looked on her. She leveled a gaze at herself in the mirror and reminded herself this was all for the greater good. Better this than having to marry Mr. Dallweather. Bonnets were just another weapon of war.

So with campaign on her mind, Brynnde marched downstairs to meet Julia and Eleanor. "Mama is in the carriage," Julia said breezily. "Once she is fixed, it is impossible to unstick her."

They waited some minutes for Tessa, who eventually

came flying down the stairs in pale pink and a surfeit of lace. Then they all scrambled aboard the barouche, Brynnde and Eleanor next to Lady Darley while Julia was left with Tessa. Julia made such a face at them when her mother wasn't looking—an expression that comically reprimanded Brynnde and Eleanor for abandoning her to Tessa —that it was all Brynnde could do to keep from laughing aloud.

This is what is must be like to have friends, Brynnde thought suddenly. *Or sisters you actually get along with.* Though she was close in many ways to her father and brother, Brynnde was so different from her mother and sister as to have grown up lacking that bond particular to female friendships and relations. It was a novel feeling, and a pleasant one.

The barouche set off and before long had joined the throng in Hyde Park. Pedestrians strolled under constant danger of being trampled by those on horseback or in carriages. It was the most colorful, incoherent crowd Brynnde had ever seen.

Because there were so many people, progress was necessarily slow, but this allowed for prolonged conversation between carriages. Brynnde lost track of the names of everyone Lady Darley introduced them to. She felt her brain fugging, her eyes glazing over until a familiar voice cut through the incessant murmuring of the mob.

"Look, Mother, who I found!" Garrick Sommerford's voice boomed, and suddenly he was beside the carriage, sitting astride a lovely blood bay. He noticed Brynnde at the moment she recognized him, raised his brows and tipped his hat. "And you've found someone yourself, I see."

"Oh, Garrick, we told you last night at dinner—" Julia began.

"Did you? But look, here is our own Mr. Dryer all the way from Oakesgrove." A shy-looking young man with hair somewhere between brown and red rode forward hesitantly on what Brynnde suspected was a hired horse. He looked impossibly young, but his brown eyes shone when they landed on Eleanor. As for Eleanor, she could not keep the blood out of her cheeks at the sight of him.

"Why, Mr. Dryer!" cried Lady Darley. "Whatever are you doing in London? Business, I'm sure," she answered without giving him a chance to. "However all that works." She waved a hand in seeming dismissal.

Garrick's lips twisted in something like amusement. "Misses Archambault," he said, "may I present Mr. Thomas Dryer." Brynnde nodded to Mr. Dryer, but Tessa only stared, eyes narrowed in thought.

"I believe Mr. Dryer will be at the Tomington party next week," Garrick went on gamely.

This caught Lady Darley's attention. "Really? How do you know the Tomingtons, Mr. Dryer? Oh, business again," she sighed. "It's no use telling me about it."

Julia's eyes met Brynnde's and they each had to bite their lips to keep from giggling. Poor Mr. Dryer had yet to tell anyone about anything! And no wonder; he had eyes only for Eleanor. Brynnde wondered whether he'd heard anything they'd said.

"Well then," Garrick said with another tip of his hat. "We'll be off." He started to turn his horse only to be stopped by his mother.

"But where is Graeme?" Lady Darley asked abruptly.

"Haven't a clue," said Garrick, and Brynnde thought he grimaced but she couldn't be certain.

The remainder of their outing became a blur of names and faces. Brynnde reminded herself she needed to take things seriously if she didn't want to be stuck with Mr. Dall-weather, but though there were any number of eligible men, and some of them were even handsome, she felt too over-whelmed to take note of anyone in particular.

Brynnde watched Julia and Tessa with interest, however. Each of them was extremely selective about her interactions with the gentlemen who stopped to chat with them. Oh, they were always polite but only sometimes warm. Brynnde wondered what made the difference and resolved to ask Julia when she had the chance. Eleanor, on the other hand, seemed out of sorts when called upon to acknowledge or respond to anyone. Her dreamy gaze continually turned in the direction Garrick and Mr. Dryer had gone.

The driver was turning the barouche toward Berkeley Square when Nicolas rode up. Brynnde couldn't help smiling at the sight of her handsome brother, made all the more dashing by his new London clothes. Even better, he was completely unaware of the figure he cut. Unlike so many other men who swaggered and puffed, Nicolas did not have it in him to show off. He was only ever wholly himself.

As Nicolas complimented everyone, Brynnde noticed something else. Though Julia had given her attention to a number of young men that afternoon, she was practically riveted on Nicolas, her eyes fixed avidly on his face. A thought sparked in the back of Brynnde's brain. She looked to Eleanor, who seemed not to have noticed, but then she wouldn't have noticed if a bird landed to nest on her head at that point. All Eleanor's thoughts were bent in only one direction.

So Brynnde looked to Lady Darley. That robust woman conversed quite gamely with Nicolas, her eyes sliding now and then toward her eldest daughter. It was the most engaged Brynnde had observed the matron to be, leaving

Brynnde to wonder whether Lady Darley was promoting the match (meaning Julia was only being dutiful in paying such attention to Nicolas), or vice versa. Had Julia hit upon Nicolas and Lady Darley taken up her cause?

Brynnde eyed her brother speculatively. Did he know? Did he hold Julia in any particular esteem? Impossible to tell. Nicolas was equally polite and outgoing toward everyone.

Nicolas escorted the barouche back to Berkeley Square, and as soon as the Sommerfords were filled with promises to visit and away, Brynnde sprang on him. "What do you make of Julia Darley?" she asked as they made their way upstairs.

Her brother gave a light laugh. "Which one is she? I can't tell them apart."

Brynnde looked sharply at him in attempt to determine whether he was being truthful or trying to cover his feelings. "She's the older one. The one who actually talks."

"Oh," said Nicolas, "yes, she's actually quite sharp, isn't she? Witty, I mean, but not in a mean way."

It was, Brynnde reflected, the nicest thing she'd ever heard him say about any young lady outside of, "She's very pretty." Many girls were pretty, but few of those were also sharp and witty. It sounded promising.

Brynnde came at him from another direction. "What do you suppose her chances are this Season?"

Nicolas turned a startled face toward her as they stopped on the landing. "How should I know? Though if her brother..." He shook his head and pressed his lips together.

"Gar—I mean, Lord Burbridge?" Brynnde asked.

Her brother's eyes narrowed at her. "You almost called him by his Christian name," he accused. "But no. I meant

The Honourable Graeme." He made Graeme sound anything but honourable.

"I thought you liked Mr. Sommerford. The two of you were quite companionable at the house party."

Nicolas grimaced in much the same way Brynnde fancied Garrick had done. She could see her brother shuttering himself, reining in his response. Whatever Graeme Sommerford was up to, Nicolas did not feel it was fit for her to hear about it. "I do like him," Nicolas admitted. "He's not altogether an idiot. But every man has his stupid moments," he added.

"He's done something stupid?" Brynnde asked.

But Nicolas was already turning away toward his room. "I smell like the stables. I need to get out of these clothes and into something for dinner."

He left Brynnde staring after him, chewing her lip in consideration.

8

The following week came the Tomingtons' party. "The cream of the Ton will be there," Maman declared as they settled into the carriage. "Lady Tomington is extremely particular about her guest lists."

Brynnde almost asked how, if that were the case, they'd ended up with an invitation then thought better of it. Maman clearly had no tolerance for jokes at the moment. Her expression was most severe as she looked at Tessa. "This is not an opportunity to be squandered."

She must mean the house party, Brynnde thought. Both Tessa and Maman had been gravely disappointed that it had not ended with a proposal. And if Tessa could not accomplish it in a week's time, how would she accomplish it in one night?

And what about you? Brynnde asked herself. She nearly laughed aloud, but managed to make it come out more like a cough. No, she did not expect to wrangle a proposal from anyone that night, but she knew she must at least begin catching eyes.

Maman's shrewd countenance swung her way. "Not falling ill, are you?"

"No, Maman," said Brynnde. "It's only this London air."

Maman sniffed. "We want to have a good report for your father when he arrives at the end of the month." By which Brynnde assumed she meant a bouquet of serious, respectable suitors, if not an offer already in hand.

The carriage rolled to a stop and one of the Tomingtons' hired men handed the ladies down and gestured them into the imposing mansion. "Who *are* the Tomingtons anyway?" Brynnde whispered to Tessa.

Tessa snorted. "Lord David Moncrieff is Earl of Tomington, but his wife is Duchess of Laybornne. She's very—Oh! There she is."

They were announced and made their curtsies under the duchess' cool, gray gaze. The woman was tall and thin, and her ice blue gown made her appear all the colder. Brynnde saw her as a kind of fencepost, a boundary marker.

The duchess nodded to Lady Averland, looked over Tessa and gave another nod. Then she scrutinized Brynnde, and one carefully plucked eyebrow lifted. After what felt like an eternity, the duchess nodded again, and they were released, free to join the party.

Brynnde finally asked the question that had occurred to her during their carriage ride. "How did we even manage an invitation?"

"I believe my mother may have had something to do with it," said a voice from behind her.

Brynnde turned and scowled at Garrick Sommerford. "You really must stop creeping up behind people," she scolded. But the twinkle in his eye prevented her from staying angry. He took her gloved hand and gave it a practiced kiss then examined her dance card.

"It's empty!"

"We only just arrived."

"Then I am fortunate to have first choice." He took the tiny pencil and wrote in his name. Catching Tessa's blazing glare, he smiled and said, "May I, Miss Archambault?"

Tessa's distemper melted immediately into a simpering smile as she offered him her card. Garrick dutifully signed.

"I will see you for the first dance," Garrick told Brynnde as Lady Averland clucked like a mother hen and urged her girls onward.

Brynnde surreptitiously glanced at her card as they maneuvered through the gathering. Yes, Garrick had selected the first *and* last dances of the evening, the last one being a closing waltz.

Soon came another dizzying array of introductions. Brynnde reminded herself to smile and tried to take interest in the gentlemen signing her dance card, but it felt to her like a parade of strange birds. Some strutted, some shied, and they came in any number of shapes and colors.

As the evening progressed, Brynnde concluded most birds were better enjoyed at a distance. A number of the gentlemen were only marginally acquainted with dancing; more still were barely capable of conversation. At least three of them expended the majority of their energy attempting to look down Brynnde's gown.

Duchess or no duchess, the night could not end soon enough. And then Garrick appeared at Brynnde's elbow.

"You look surprised," he remarked. "I did sign for the last waltz, I believe?"

Brynnde let out a sigh of relief. "It's over!"

Garrick's mouth twitched. "Almost. You haven't enjoyed yourself?"

All at once, without knowing why, Brynnde poured out

the entire story, from Mr. Dallweather's proposal to her father's ultimatum. "A bird in the hand indeed!" she finished. "They can all stay in the bushes!"

For a brief moment, Garrick appeared shocked, and in that second Brynnde wished she hadn't told him any of it. Why had she? They weren't particular friends, after all. She looked away, searching for something else to talk about. But before she could ask how Eleanor and Mr. Dryer were getting on, Garrick said, "Birds now? Last time they were stones."

The first strains of the waltz began, and Garrick took Brynnde's hand and placed it on his arm. "There is another option," he said.

Brynnde turned her miserable face to his. "Run away?"

"All right, then there are two other options," Garrick amended.

"What is the other one?" Brynnde asked.

"You could marry me."

Brynnde almost stopped dancing, but Garrick skillfully guided her through the continued steps.

"You... You hardly know me!" said Brynnde.

"Then tell me what you think I should know," he said. When she only stared, he went on, "You love to ride, you're a fine dancer and archer, you prefer the countryside to town, and Mother says you have a good head on your shoulders."

"Oh, well, if your mother says so."

Garrick smiled. "And you have a sharp wit."

Something else occurred to Brynnde. "Why would your mother be talking about me?"

"Why do women talk about anyone?" Garrick countered. The waltz was ending. He said, "You still haven't given me your answer."

Brynnde studied him, the too tan face and angelic hair

belied by storm cloud eyes. "It could work," she mused. "You would almost never be home anyway."

For the second time that evening, Garrick Sommerford appeared taken aback. "No, you're right, I do travel quite a bit." The words sounded uncharacteristically tentative, a gentle probe.

"Ridgemow is not Aux Arbres, but I'm sure I could love it," Brynnde continued thoughtfully.

This time Garrick did not respond, merely waited.

Brynnde met his gaze and nodded. "I accept your offer."

"I'll add that to the list," said Garrick as he led Brynnde from the dance floor.

"What?" Brynnde asked.

"That you're an astute woman of business."

LORD AVERLAND CAME to London forthwith to begin negotiations. But first thing upon arriving he called Brynnde to him in the library. She stood on the carpet and waited, but her father only stared at her as if waiting for her to recite a lesson. Finally, she was moved to ask, "What is it, Papa?"

"I want to be sure, before we get too far into this, that *you* are sure," he said. "It is, after all, rather sudden." He squinted a little as though to see her better somehow. "Is this a whirlwind passion, hm? The two of you fell in love at first sight?"

Brynnde wasn't sure which her father would find worse —her falling in love so abruptly or her being unemotional and businesslike about it. She hedged by saying, "He's actually quite charming."

"Snakes are charming, but still they bite. You've known Dallweather much longer," Lord Averland noted. "You know the kind of man he is. What if Burbridge—" He paused and pursed his lips as Brynnde started visibly at his use of Garrick's title. "Has he encouraged familiarity? No? Well, he's still Lord Burbridge to the rest of us. What if he turns out to be some kind of brute? Hm?"

It hadn't occurred to Brynnde that such things might worry her father. "I'm certain he isn't," she said, though she had a mental flash of those iron eyes, could all too easily picture them hardened with ire.

"They're a good family," Lord Averland conceded, "and I like Lord Darley very much. Tessa must be in a lather," he added half to himself. "She so had it in her head to get herself a title."

"Lord Burbridge," Brynnde began, and found it strange how difficult it was to make her tongue form the name, "is not the only eligible man in London with a title."

Lord Averland harrumphed. "True enough. Well, if you're sure," and he paused again to allow Brynnde to change her mind. When she didn't, he finished, "we will begin the arrangements. But let's not rush anything, yes? Do you have a date in mind?"

Brynnde had not thought that far ahead. "Oh, after the Season," she said and hoped Garrick would be agreeable to that.

"We'll plan for September," said her father, seemingly satisfied. He came around the library table that he used for work while in London, placed his hands on her shoulders, and kissed her forehead. "I only want what is best for you, you know. And I want you to be happy."

Brynnde longed to tell him she would be happy only if he let her remain at Aux Arbres. But she knew he would not be moved. She suspected that, just sometimes, what was best for a person and what made them happy were two very different, incompatible things.

9

____

After the initial shock—how had her most difficult child become the one to land a titled fiancé while her loveliest daughter remained unattached?—Lady Averland began the arrangements. The trousseau, the breakfast... The Sommerfords would get the license, and a church must be agreed upon...

Brynnde envisioned the long, hot summer that stretched ahead, filled with more trips to the dressmaker and so many social engagements, and wished more than ever to be in the quiet of Aux Arbres. She'd done her part, found a man willing to marry her, so why could she not now retire to the country and be done?

Still, she could not help but be happy when Lady Darley and her daughters came to visit. "Sisters!" Eleanor cried without preamble. "We shall be sisters now!"

Julia's green eyes slid over the room. "Where's the other one? Nursing her wounded pride?"

Brynnde understood she meant Tessa. "She has been sulking," Brynnde admitted. "And I spend every meal with her looking daggers into me." She sought to change the subject, and looking to Eleanor asked, "And what of you and Mr. Dryer?" They'd met again briefly at supper at the Tomingtons' ball but Brynnde had otherwise been too occupied to chat. Handed from gentleman to gentleman like a kerchief. Well, at least she no longer need endure that.

Eleanor bit her lip, leaving Julia to answer for her. "Mr. Dryer has been called home."

"But I do think he made a favorable impression on Mama!" Eleanor added, her eyes bright and fervent.

Brynnde looked to Julia for confirmation and received a tiny shake of the head.

"I'm sure he did," Brynnde said for Eleanor's sake. "But you must at least attempt to enjoy the rest of your Season in his absence."

This won her a grateful smile from Julia.

Eleanor nodded. "I will try."

"It's no sin against Mr. Dryer to have fun. He would want you to," Brynnde insisted, and Eleanor nodded again, though Brynnde fancied shadows of doubt lay over the girl's pretty features.

Lady Darley rose, and the others in the room followed suit. That *grand dame* sailed over to where Brynnde stood and smiled down at her. "My dear child, we are so happy to have you join our family."

The unexpected declaration brought tears to Brynnde's eyes and a lump to her throat. It also planted a seed of guilt in Brynnde's heart. She wasn't doing it for them, or even for Garrick. If anything, *he* was doing it for *her*, though Brynnde still could not understand why.

"Thank you," Brynnde managed, "for welcoming me so warmly."

Lady Darley gave a curt nod as if Brynnde's words satisfied something in her. "Garrick is out of town for a few days," she announced as she swept toward the door, her daughters in her wake. "As you might imagine, there is so much business now to accomplish. But he'll come to see you as soon as he returns." Her tone left no question that her son *would* do, whether he wanted to or not.

Once the guests had gone, Brynnde asked her mother, "Where is Tessa? It's not like her to ignore visitors."

"She hasn't been well," Lady Averland answered primly. "Caught something at the Tomingtons', I think."

"A case of green envy is what," Molly told Brynnde that evening as she readied her mistress for dinner.

Brynnde had to concede Molly was likely right. Ever since the engagement, Tessa had refused to go out, coming down only for meals, and only that because Maman and Papa would not allow her to eat from trays in her room. Now Maman put out word that Tessa had taken ill—nothing serious, no, just a little complaint that would surely pass—and Brynnde likewise found herself sidelined. Being she was off the marriage market, she became the subject of many whispers, forced smiles, and insincere congratulations. And while she did not entirely mind not dancing, long evenings spent in idle chatter and holding up ballroom walls were far from Brynnde's idea of enjoyment.

There were two men with which Brynnde could and did dance on occasion: her brother, and her brother-in-law to be. Nicolas seemed genuinely happy for her, if surprised by the precipitate betrothal. Looking to tweak him a bit, Brynnde said, "And if you were to marry Julia..."

To her surprise, her usually stalwart brother blushed. "What makes you think I'm even in the market? I'm young yet."

"You're here," said Brynnde, "which puts you on the market, at least in the eyes of all these mamas. And you may be young, but Papa is not." She hesitated then pressed on. "Is there anyone you've—you've found that you...?"

"I haven't thought seriously about it," said Nicolas as the dance came to an end and he returned Brynnde to their mother.

As for The Honourable Graeme Sommerford, Brynnde discovered him to be in much the same amiable, jovial mood as during their house party. She searched his countenance for any cause of Nicolas' or Garrick's disgust but came away with nothing. And though he joked lightly about wishing he'd proposed before his brother, nothing Graeme said could be taken with any real repulsion.

"You're enjoying London?" Brynnde asked him.

"Oh, very much," said Graeme. "It's always been Ridgemow, you know, so I find everything here new and exciting. Don't you?"

"It's different," Brynnde assented, but she could not bring herself to say she liked it.

"And what of your sister?" Graeme inquired. "I feel as though I have not seen her these last few occasions."

"No, she is ailing. Nothing serious," Brynnde hastened to add.

Graeme smiled in a way Brynnde did not entirely like, a way that suggested a secret. "She will recover," he said, and Brynnde was tempted to demand just what he knew about it, but she held her tongue.

Tessa, meanwhile, had begun to believe being mysteriously ill made her somehow a more romantic figure. She stayed home for a full two weeks before reappearing on the social scene. And to her delight, the mamas did fawn a bit, and all their daughters sympathized while the sons declared they were happy to see her restored and danced with her as though to wear her health down again.

Brynnde was forced to admit Tessa was more beautiful than ever. Paler, eyes feverishly bright. The gentlemen flocked around her, and while some young ladies took dislike to her, just as many sought her company. Brynnde wondered whether that was because they honestly enjoyed Tessa's acquaintance, or if they simply hoped to catch her castoff suitors.

She didn't have time to find out. Maman kept Brynnde in a whirl of plans, and whenever she could manage to get away, Brynnde found herself set upon with equal fervor by her sisters-in-law to be. But she could not be sorry for that. Eleanor required the combined efforts of both Julia and Brynnde to keep her spirits up in the absence of Mr. Dryer. And Brynnde also hoped to discover whether Julia had any particular feelings for Nicolas.

It was no easy feat. Brynnde did not possess the knack for small talk and did not know how to begin to extract the information she wanted. Eleanor opened the avenue for her when, one day as they sat in the small garden behind the townhouse, she said, "Never mind about Lord Wode dancing with me! Lord Richford was paying every kind of attention to Julia!"

Brynnde blinked owlishly and tried to remember which one was Lord Richford. "Was he?"

"And he's ever so handsome!" Eleanor went on.

"His face is too square," said Julia dismissively. "In fact, his whole body is shaped like a brick."

"You do not care for... square men?" Brynnde asked.

Julia sighed and stretched out her legs. "He is loud, too," she mused. "That booming laugh." She gave a mock shudder. "And his jokes are not clever, nor does he understand when *I* am being witty."

"So that's a definite no then," Brynnde summarized.

Julia bounded up from the bench and began to turn agitated circles. "He has a fine title, but his home is a pile of rock. I suspect he spends his money on—" She waved a hand. "Not his estate, and probably not his wife, either."

Eleanor turned to Brynnde. "Mama is pursuing the match," she explained.

"Why?" Brynnde asked.

Julia plopped back down onto the bench. "Because it would be a social triumph."

"Surely there must be any number of eligible men who would count as such," said Brynnde. She remembered saying something similar to Papa about Tessa's options as well.

Julia shrugged and began to fidget with the cuff of her dress. Brynnde knew it was the moment to ask.

"Is there someone else you prefer?"

Julia's green eyes flew to Brynnde's face, wide with an odd mixture of apprehension and defiance. "I am not like Ellie, pining for a mere merchant!"

Eleanor rocked back where she sat as if struck by a physical blow. Immediately Julia apologized. "I'm sorry, Ellie, really. I just..." She twisted her hands in her lap and took a deep breath. "There is someone—but he has not noticed me."

"You've been introduced?" Brynnde asked.

Julia nodded.

"Danced?" Brynnde pressed.

"Once or twice," Julia admitted. Then she threw up her hands. "But he only does it out of duty!"

"How do you know?" asked Brynnde. "He's said this to you?"

Julia rounded on her. "Of course not! But he hasn't..." Her brow puckered. "He's barely spoken to me!"

"Perhaps he is shy," Brynnde suggested, "or isn't sure of your interest either."

"It's a wonder anyone manages to marry!" Julia cried, throwing her hands up once more. She cocked her head at Brynnde like a curious bird. "How did you and my brother accomplish so quick a proposal?"

Heat flooded Brynnde's cheeks. "It *was* sudden," she conceded. She could hardly tell them their brother had offered for her out of pity for her situation.

"That's Garrick for you, though," said Julia. "Never one to wait when it comes to something he wants."

Eleanor stirred where she sat. "Julia wishes she'd been born a man," she told Brynnde. "Then she wouldn't have to wait either."

"Tell us who it is," said Brynnde abruptly, and again Julia's eyes went wide. "Maybe we can... urge him to speak." She had no idea how to accomplish such a thing, but it was worth a try. And she was devilishly curious about this mystery man.

Julia leaned forward slightly and looked across Brynnde to where Eleanor sat. Eleanor gave an encouraging nod. Then Julia sat back and looked at Brynnde warily. "It is your brother."

Brynnde only just contained her whoop of delight, turning it into a hacking cough that had Julia staring in horror. "I knew I shouldn't have told you!"

"No! No, really," Brynnde said once she was able to speak. "This actually makes it so much easier. Because I do believe Nicolas holds you in esteem as well."

Now Julia looked at Brynnde as if she'd gone mad.

"He just—he hasn't yet come to the conclusion he needs a wife," Brynnde went on. "He's only twenty-four, after all. But he speaks to you, Julia, more than any other young lady of his acquaintance. That must count for something."

Brynnde could see from Julia's expression that she scarce dared to hope Nicolas might have noticed her. But that she *wanted* to hope more than anything.

"I can talk to him—" Brynnde began.

Julia leapt to her feet again. "No! You can't tell him!"

Brynnde was spared having to respond by a leonine figure emerging from the townhouse. Eleanor, first to spot him, smiled widely. "You're back!"

Garrick bowed to them. "I am. And I've brought something for my fiancée." He looked meaningfully at Brynnde, slate eyes gleaming, and offered his hand to help her to her feet.

"Brought something? From where?" Brynnde asked. The words came automatically; meanwhile, Julia worked to catch Brynnde's eye, her face a mask of worry. Brynnde gave the girl a small nod to show she understood and would not say anything to Nicolas about Julia's professed interest in him.

"From home," said Garrick. "Your home, to be precise."

They strolled together around to the mews where the horses and carriage were stabled. Brynnde could not imagine what Garrick wanted to show her there, and Julia and Eleanor exchanged glances that told her they also did not understand. But then a deep snort sounded, and a glossy black head emerged from one of the stalls.

"Parnassus!" Brynnde cried. She flung her arms around the horse's neck, and Parnassus snuffled her hair affectionately—or in search of sugar.

"Now we may ride together in Hyde Park," said Garrick.

They could have done that even without Parnassus, but the fact Garrick had fetched her favorite horse over-whelmed Brynnde so that for a moment she couldn't speak. "That would be lovely," she finally managed. She looked at her fiancé, tears of gratitude frustratingly close to the surface of her eyes. "This was the business you left town for?"

"Among other things. As you can imagine, there is much to arrange, and it cannot all be done from London." Garrick turned to his sisters. "And *you* will be happy to know Mr. Dryer is home and well."

Eleanor smiled, but Julia said, "Not too well, I hope." And when Eleanor frowned at her, Julia explained, "You don't want him to think he can be happy without you!"

Garrick laughed then looked with sympathy at his youngest sister. "You know Mother will never agree to it, Ellie."

Eleanor's green eyes filled with tears. "But—but you have made a respectable match, and Julia—" The flash of Julia's eyes stopped her from elaborating there. "And Graeme will surely... Why shouldn't I marry Mr. Dryer?" she wailed. "It could hardly matter what I do!"

Garrick placed a hand on her shoulder. "It does matter. For all of us. The people we tie ourselves to... It matters," he said again, lamely.

"And anyway Graeme—" Julia began, but Garrick rounded on her, face like a thundercloud and eyes blazing lightning. Julia swallowed her words and lowered her gaze to her shoes.

Brynnde observed this with interest. Julia knew something about whatever Graeme was up to. Heady with the success of having extracted the truth of Julia's interest in Nicolas, Brynnde determined to next ply her skill in that direction.

"Well then," Garrick said, too brightly, "it's about time

we take our leave." He smiled at Brynnde but she saw the tightness around his eyes. "We shall see you this afternoon for our ride?"

Brynnde nodded, patting Parnassus again. "I'll be back with carrots," she promised. Then she took her fiancé's proffered arm and allowed him to lead them back into the house, all pretending as if nothing were wrong, no, nothing at all.

10

———

As so often was the case, the scandal, when it came, did not rain down so much as erupt from beneath Brynnde's feet. It began with glances and whispers whenever she went out, be it to shops, or on social calls, or at the endless blur of parties that dominated her evenings. Oh, everyone still smiled and behaved politely towards her, but Brynnde was astute enough to recognize pity when it flickered behind people's eyes. Her triumph at landing the oldest son of an earl became mutters of, "There but by the grace of God..."

This went on for over a week. Brynnde and Garrick continued to meet at the numerous balls, but he had ceased to ask her to ride with him in Hyde Park. Maman, too, no longer ushered Brynnde from shop to shop in preparation for the wedding. Something, she realized, was very wrong.

Then Lord Averland called Brynnde to the library again. As she passed the drawing room, she could hear Tessa screeching, "And now her poor choice will taint me, too!" For a moment Brynnde swayed in that direction, but the thought of Tessa's sneer stopped her. She continued on to the library.

"Brynnde," her father said with a heavy sigh, "I'm afraid your engagement is at an end."

Brynnde felt behind her for the solidity of the library door to prop her up. "What? Why?"

"There are some things I'd rather you not know," Lord Archambault said. "And for that reason, I am sending all of you back to Aux Arbres."

Brynnde's heart fluttered. She should be happy— thrilled—to return home. Yet she could not be, not wholly, without knowing the reason. Her curiosity hung over her like a cloud over the sun.

"But if we go home, how will Tessa find a husband?" Brynnde asked. "And will I be expected to marry Mr. Dall-weather?"

"You'd be happier with him than with any of these swains and dandies," snapped her father. "You cannot know that, of course, you haven't had the experience, but in the long run, he'd be far better for you." Lord Averland took a look at his daughter's stricken face and added, grudgingly, "But I won't force you to accept him. Not right away at any rate.

"Go on up and get packed," he went on.

"Now?" asked Brynnde.

"Yes, yes!" Lord Averland made a shooing motion. "I will remain in town to tidy up a few ends, but the rest of you are to pack and be ready to leave first thing."

A few ends. One major end, at least, Brynnde thought as she trudged upstairs, her mind reeling. Was she sorry? Yes, she supposed she was. The feeling surprised her. But though she had no great passion for Garrick, he'd been amenable, easy to talk to, even fun at times. She pictured the way his eyes crinkled when he smiled (which was often) and felt as though, more than losing a future husband, she was losing a friend.

It was Graeme, of course. Whatever he'd been mixed up in—that had to be what had brought everything to such shambles.

Instead of turning right toward her room, Brynnde turned left and went to knock on her brother's door. "Nicolas?"

It took so long for him to answer Brynnde began to think he might not be home. She was turning away to leave when at last the door clicked open. Brynnde could just see past him into a room strewn with garments; Nicolas loved clothes far more than Brynnde and almost as much as Tessa.

"Are you packing?" Brynnde asked.

Nicolas glanced over his shoulder. "Martin will do it."

Nicolas' poor valet. "I suppose this means we're not going to the Wickershams' tonight," said Brynnde.

Her brother sighed. "You want to know what happened," he guessed, "and Father won't tell you."

Brynnde rewarded him with a smile, but Nicolas only shook his head. "I don't... can't..."

"It's Graeme, isn't it?" Brynnde said, stepping into her brother's faltering silences.

Nicolas turned to look up and down the hall, making sure no servants were around. Then he pulled Brynnde into his room and shut the door. "What have you heard?" he asked sternly.

His severe expression startled Brynnde. She could count on one hand the times in her life she'd seen her brother truly angry or upset. "Nothing," she said earnestly. "But Ga —Lord Burbridge would sometimes get this look on his face whenever Graeme's name was mentioned, and you said—"

"I never said anything," Nicolas inserted abruptly.

"You said he was stupid," Brynnde countered.

"So are a lot of people," said Nicolas. "It doesn't end engagements. Usually," he added with a grimace.

"What did he do?" Brynnde asked plaintively.

But Nicolas shook his head again. "It's nothing you need to know about. In fact, it's the kind of thing nice ladies don't know about."

Brynnde rolled her eyes. "So I'm a nice lady now?"

Nicolas grinned. "Very proper."

Brynnde took a couple of mincing steps and batted her eyes. Nicolas laughed then stopped when he saw his sister's calculating expression. "You're thinking about whom else you could ask," he accused.

Brynnde's eyebrows went up.

"Brynnde..." Nicolas warned.

"Maybe I'll send a note directly round to Lord Burbridge," she suggested.

"You know you can't!"

"I know I *shouldn't*. I absolutely *can*."

Nicolas tilted his head back and squeezed his eyes shut. He drew in a deep breath. "I will *not* give you details," he began, and Brynnde knew she had won. "Graeme..." He sought the most delicate words. "Compromised a young lady... who was not yet out."

Brynnde could not hide her dismay. To compromise a lady was bad enough, but one so young?

"That is all I will say," Nicolas went on resolutely, "and more than you should know."

Brynnde turned blindly for the door, managed to get it open on the third try. She half stumbled back to her room, almost failed to make it to the bed before she sat.

Oh, yes, bad indeed. To be connected even slightly with such a scandal! But how much worse it must be for Julia and Eleanor... and for Garrick.

A voice inside Brynnde told her Garrick would be fine regardless. He would travel abroad and polish himself anew from this tarnish. His sisters would not have that luxury.

Yet Brynnde found herself thinking of Garrick all the same. She pictured those eyes again, no longer in good humor but instead flashing lightning through the stormy gray of them. She shivered, glad his anger was not directed at her but Graeme.

And what of Graeme? And the poor girl he'd compromised? They would have to marry, despite her age. Heavens, what a mess!

There came a pounding up the stairs and a stomping down the corridor. Tessa in a froth over her ruined chances. Brynnde considered going to her, trying to talk to her, but dismissed the idea almost immediately. To do so would only give Tessa a chance to throw things and screech some more.

Slowly, dazedly, Brynnde stood and went to her wardrobe, began pulling out the clothes in order to pack them. She did not ring for Molly, preferring to be alone as a rainbow of gowns collected on the bed. So many that she might never have a chance to wear, and though Brynnde did not generally obsess over fashion, she did lament the wasted expense.

Matching bonnets joined the dresses, and Brynnde knew Molly would bewail their lack of boxes keeping them in good form. Gloves, slippers... Brynnde's bed became a mountain of garments rivaling Madame Odille's showroom.

A tap on the door broke Brynnde's rhythm, and all at once she was exhausted, as though cleaning out her wardrobe had cleaned out something in herself as well. Without answering the knock, Brynnde flung herself onto the pile and began, finally, to cry.

11

The sorrow was not so much for lost love—there was, in Brynnde's mind, no love to lose. But her heart broke over the setback her revoked engagement dealt her. She could only be grateful her father would not demand she marry Mr. Dallweather, at least not for the moment.

And her friendships! Those *were* lost, fragile and new and now gone like dandelion fluff in a strong wind. Julia and Eleanor, the handful of other young ladies she'd come to know over the weeks... All severed from her in one swift swing of the social sword.

No, she did not love London, but for the first time in Brynnde's life the thought of Aux Arbres brought her little joy. Instead it stood for isolation, shame, and potentially ultimate defeat.

The tap came again and this time the door opened without waiting for an answer. Molly eased into the room, quiet and timid. "Oh, Miss," she said when Brynnde looked up red-eyed from the heap of clothing, "I am that sorry for all what's happened."

Brynnde heaved herself upright and swiped at her eyes. "Leave one dress for dinner and one for tomorrow," she instructed dully. "I don't care which."

Molly sighed over the gowns and Brynnde drifted out of the room, unable to tolerate the presence of another body inside her bubble of misery. As she wandered out to the garden, she wished she might at least send Julia and Eleanor a note of some kind, but of course she could not. Even if they met again—which was unlikely enough—they would not be allowed to continue their former friendship. *Sister*ship. Brynnde would be forced to remain solemn and aloof.

She settled on the bench and welcomed the warmth of the sun slanting over her. The Sommerfords were of high rank, Brynnde reminded herself. They would overcome this scandal. A year or two, as Papa had said. Graeme, well *he* might not be accepted again in some circles, but Brynnde assumed his family would closet him in the country and leave him there to become an old story that passed from whispers to vague recollection.

A wonder occurred to Brynnde then. Graeme would have to marry the girl, wouldn't he? Would he take her to Ridgemow? Or maybe the girl's family was wealthy and would provide a place as dowry. They'd snared the younger son of an earl after all, so they could hardly complain.

Brynnde shook off her idle curiosities with a toss of her dark curls. How jaded London had made her! Perhaps it was just as well she would be going home to Aux Arbres and getting away from the influences of the Season.

Whoever the girl might be, she was surely frightened and embarrassed and—

A rustling among the trees that divided the garden from the mews pulled Brynnde from her musings. She scanned the foliage but saw nothing. A squirrel perhaps? Brynnde stood to look only to catch the glint of blond hair in the sunlight.

"Garrick!" she gasped, not thinking quickly enough to keep from using his Christian name.

He stepped around the tree and smiled, though only with one side of his mouth. The corners of his eyes were pinched with apprehension.

Brynnde stole a glance at the house in hopes no one was looking out a window or coming to find her. Garrick needlessly put a finger to his lips to indicate she should stay quiet —as if she didn't know!—and then beckoned her to join him in the shade of the trees. With another quick look at the house, Brynnde stepped carefully into the sheltering branches.

"I'm sorry," Garrick said without preamble. "I know I shouldn't be here, but I hated to..." He made a gesture meant to fill in for the words, though Brynnde could not entirely translate it. "The best laid plans, eh?" he finished with a tiny shrug and a wavering smile.

Brynnde swallowed hard against the unexpected lump that swelled in her throat. "We leave in the morning," she said. "I'm only sorry not to be able to say goodbye to Julia and Eleanor. I'll miss them." She bit her lip against the admission and peered up at Garrick from beneath her lashes. This was the man she'd planned to spend her life with, but "planned" was hardly the word for it. She hadn't actually given it much thought. He'd been an answer to a problem, but looking at him now she wondered what it would have been like to share a life with him.

"I'll give them your regards," said Garrick. He flexed a fist. "I could cheerfully murder Graeme." Then he stole a sideways glance at Brynnde. "I assume you've heard?"

"I managed to extract some of it from Nicolas," Brynnde told him. She twisted her lips against the rise of curiosity, but Garrick saw and rightfully deduced her thoughts. For the first time, his smile was genuine.

"You want to know what happened," he said.

"It's not for ladies to know," Brynnde said primly.

Garrick's smile only broadened. "I'll tell you, if you like."

Brynnde looked up sharply, then over her shoulder at the house.

"He'd become infatuated with young Lady Elisabeth Talmidge," said Garrick plainly. "Mother had been promoting a match between Graeme and Lady Elisabeth's older sister Honora, but it was the younger who caught his eye."

"And now what?"

"Lady Elisabeth will be sixteen in November. Young but..." Garrick shrugged.

"He will marry her?" Brynnde asked.

"He must. Not that he's sorry," added Garrick.

"The Talmidges must be furious," mused Brynnde, then with wide eyes added, "not that your family isn't—I mean, of course your brother is—oh, drat it!" She stamped a foot in frustration.

Garrick laughed. "Does that help your mouth work better?" When Brynnde gaped at him, he laughed again. "Apparently not." He became serious then. "The Talmidges were not best pleased at the situation, no. No more than were we. The wedding will be quiet, and it will all blow over in time. Maybe..." A speculative glimmer swam through his eyes. "If you aren't Mrs. Dallweather by then..."

Brynnde watched in a dazed and distracted sort of way as Garrick lifted his hand, not realizing what he meant to do until he ran a finger over her cheek. She knew she should pull away, but rather like a cat she felt compelled to push her cheek into the touch. "I doubt Papa would—" she began, but then a shrill call cut her words short.

"Brynnde! Brynnde, are you out here?"

"Yes, Maman!" Brynnde answered. She turned to give Garrick some hasty parting words but, like a shadow burned away by sunlight, he was already gone.

THE COUNTRYSIDE FELT fresh and cool compared to the heat and pollution of London, and Brynnde soon fell into her old habits. Lord Averland made clear he did not hold Brynnde at any fault, nor should any other member of the family. This dammed up Tessa's wailing though she continued to send Brynnde dark looks as often as she could get away with it.

Still, even if not to escape Tessa's glares, Brynnde preferred to be out riding the estate and visiting the tenants. She knew from their sympathetic looks that word had traveled fast—though how much anyone knew of what had happed was unclear, and of course none of them said anything. Brynnde was grateful not to be pressed into talking about it, but she also became increasingly uncomfortable under the scrutiny. She ceased to stay as long while visiting, making vague excuses for her sudden departures, until finally she began to pass by houses where she once would stay for long, happy afternoon chats.

Brynnde was riding home from a typical wander, feeling as though she had nowhere to go nor anywhere she much wanted to be, when the sight of a familiar carriage at the doors of Aux Arbres arrested her progress. The coach was scratched up, dusty, its paint flaking and faded—a sad picture but one that made Brynnde's heart leap. She spurred

Parnassus forward, and he readily complied, kicking up dust as they raced to greet the guests.

"Violet!" Brynnde cried, breathless, as she and Parnassus achieved the house. "What are you doing here?"

Her friend stood shyly watching the men unload her belongings while Mrs. Henderson marshaled a small army of servants to take them upstairs. At the sound of Brynnde's voice, however, Violet looked up and smiled. "Mama has been writing to your mother, and got the notion that you could do with company." The smile receded. "I hope I'm not intruding?"

"Of course not!" Brynnde swung down from her mount and rushed to give Violet a quick hug. "Oh, but," she said, drawing back. "I smell like the stable and look—" She glanced down at the clothes she'd stolen yet again. "Come inside, get settled while I change. Then you can tell me all about what I missed at the end of the Season." She motioned one of the grooms to take care of Parnassus and ushered her friend indoors.

Once changed, Brynnde met with Violet in the parlour only to find her usually timid friend turning circles like a caged tiger. "Why, Violet!" Brynnde exclaimed. "What has you so agitated?"

Violet turned a strained smile to Brynnde. "It is only want of fresh air after that coach. I think London spoiled me for being indoors!"

Brynnde understood the desire well enough and suggested they take a stroll in the garden behind the house. Violet readily agreed.

"How was London?" Brynnde asked as they marched along the path between the late roses, chrysanthemums, and asters.

"I enjoyed it more than I thought I would," Violet

admitted with a rueful twist to her lips. Brynnde felt her breath stop in her lungs, sure that Violet was about to announce an engagement. What else but love would have made London so palatable to her?

The cold stab of jealousy took Brynnde by surprise. She loved Violet and of course wanted her friend to be happy. Yet seeing Violet married also threw Brynnde's situation into high relief via contrast. For Brynnde was home at Aux Arbres, her only prospect an elderly dog lover; no wedded bliss appeared to loom in her future.

Then Violet said, "Of course, Mama is in a fit that I did not make a match, and Papa is frothing over the expense of it all, but..." She looked up at the sky wistfully. "The libraries, the museums, the parks..."

Brynnde let out a long breath. Violet wasn't in love with a man! Brynnde's relief caused her to laugh aloud. "You would marry London if you could!"

Violet squinted as if giving it serious consideration. "I would like to have a house in London," she decided. "Though I would also want the quiet of the country sometimes, too."

"Then you had better find someone wealthy after all," said Brynnde. She regarded her friend. "You met no one who struck you as amenable enough?"

Violet sniffed. "Most of them are such—such dandies! And then there are the ones who go on about hunting... Can you imagine? Killing animals for sport? Oh, they are all just so *pleased* with themselves," she finished. "I cannot imagine spending more than an hour in any of their companies, much less the rest of my life!"

Brynnde pondered the various men she'd become acquainted with while in London. Her engagement coming so early in the Season, she'd had only the most fleeting interactions with them, all very proper and staid. Even still, she had difficulty imagining Violet getting on with any of them. Not a book reader in the bunch.

Poor Violet. Her situation wasn't so far removed from Brynnde's own after all. Maybe they would both live at home as spinsters under the sufferance of their respective brothers. There were worse fates.

The specter of Mr. Dallweather rose in Brynnde's mind and she shivered. Worse fates indeed.

"Are you cold?" Violet asked, peering at her companion. "You look as though you've just seen a ghost!"

"Of the future maybe," murmured Brynnde. More robustly, she answered, "I'm only hungry. Shall we go in for tea?"

Violet agreed, and inside they went only to be greeted with, in Brynnde's opinion, the greatest of horrors.

Mr. Dallweather stood waiting in the hall.

12

———

There was no escape; he'd heard them coming.

Brynnde had no knack for disguising her feelings; she could not smile at someone she despised, and in this case she could not keep her mouth from falling open and the blood from heating her cheeks at the unexpected sight of her would-be suitor. Indeed, she stood like the veriest idiot, gaping, until Violet nudged her.

"Oh!" said Brynnde.

Mr. Dallweather made a bow. "Miss Archambault."

It took Brynnde yet another moment to remember she should introduce him to Violet, which she did. Mr. Dallweather made another bow and seemed about to speak when Jemmings arrived to save them all. "Lord Averland will see you in his study," the butler told their guest, and with yet another bow Mr. Dallweather was led away.

Brynnde all but shoved Violet in the other direction, eager for the sanctuary of the drawing room on the opposite side of the house. "I'll ring for tea."

"My word, Brynnde, you must be hungry! I've never seen you so out of sorts."

And so Brynnde found herself pouring the story out to Violet—Mr. Dallweather's offer, her father's ultimatum, and how her collapsed engagement to Garrick had put her right back where she'd started.

Violet nodded sympathetically over her tea. "I am sure he is too much a gentleman to press his suit, especially as you are still recovering from your broken engagement."

"Then why is he here?" Brynnde asked. She winced at the shrillness of her own voice; she sounded like Tessa.

"He is a friend of your father's..." Violet ventured.

"Not particularly," said Brynnde. "They have little in common. Mr. Dallweather owns a little land northeast of ours, but..." She wanted so badly to believe that could be the reason for Mr. Dallweather's visit, but the clenching in her stomach told her otherwise.

Violet did her best. "There then. That's a perfectly valid reason for a visit. Perhaps there is something to discuss about property, or crops, or difficulties with tenants." She sounded so hopeful about possible problems that Brynnde couldn't help but laugh.

After a time, the sound of Lord Averland's study door opening, the murmur of voices, and the tread of feet across the entry dampened Brynnde's and Violet's amusement. Each of them fell silent, straining her ears for any hint of what Mr. Dallweather had come to accomplish. But there only came the sound of his farewell as Jemmings opened the door for him.

Reflexively, Brynnde's gaze swung to the windows where Mr. Dallweather appeared on his way down the side path that would take him back toward Belle Weather. He strode with purpose, and Brynnde had to admit he was energetic for his age and seemingly fit.

Violet clearly was thinking along similar lines, for she said, "He's not *so* bad."

Brynnde turned to her friend, astounded. "He's healthy, and he's kind, but oh! Violet, he's so old!"

Violet shrugged. "I don't think age matters so much as a companionship of spirit."

"What do you mean?"

Violet chewed her lip for a moment as she formulated her answer. "So long as two people get along and are comfortable in one another's company... Well, it's like a friendship. There are friends you sincerely enjoy, with whom you can be truly yourself and at ease, not always worrying about propriety... The kind of person who, when you're in the room with them, it doesn't matter whether you talk because just being together is enough. Oh, I'm making a hash of it, I know," she went on. "I'm no good at articulating these things. It's something you know when you see it and feel it."

Brynnde thought of Julia and Eleanor—and, yes, Garrick—how easy it had been to spend time with them. "When it's not a chore," she said.

"Yes, that's it," Violet said with a nod. "Leave it to you to put it so succinctly."

"Even better when you actually look forward to it," Brynnde mused.

"You must miss him terribly," Violet said quietly.

"What?" Brynnde asked, distracted from her thoughts.

"Lord Burbridge. You looked so sad just then, I thought..."

In telling Violet the story, Brynnde had not emphasized that Garrick had only offered for her as a means for her to escape Mr. Dallweather. After all, that would not be fair to Garrick, letting such a thing be known. But it clearly left Violet under the impression theirs had been a love match.

"I am sad," Brynnde realized. It surprised her. She had been looking forward to joining the Sommerford family. Not only to having Julia and Eleanor as sisters, but also to spending more time with Garrick. He made her laugh, and Brynnde always felt completely at ease to be herself around him. Around all the Sommerfords.

"He would have almost never been home anyway," Brynnde reminded herself. To Violet's furrowed brow, she explained, "He prefers to travel than to stay at Ridgemow."

"Wouldn't you go with him?" Violet asked.

"Oh, I don't think so," said Brynnde. "We never really discussed it, but I'm sure he wouldn't have wanted to drag me all over the world with him like so much luggage."

"I'd rather stay here," Violet sighed. "In England, I mean. At least here I know what to expect, and what's expected of me. Out there," she waved a hand, "I'd always be lost and confused."

Brynnde was of the opinion Violet was often lost and confused even at home in England, but then that was part of her charm. She only needed to find the right kind of man to see that. Someone like...

"Violet," Brynnde said suddenly, "how do you feel about dogs?"

After dinner that evening, Lord Averland asked Brynnde to stay behind with him while everyone else left to chat and, if Maman had her way, play cards. Brynnde remained perched on the edge of her chair, hands folded together in her lap, nervous as a bird.

"Mr. Dallweather came this morning," her father began.

"I—"

He held up a hand. "I told him it was yet too soon as you were still getting over your broken engagement."

Relief and gratitude flooded Brynnde. She would have jumped up and hugged her father but his serious expression informed her he had more to say. She stayed put.

"I can't put him off forever. Christmas at the latest, and that's stretching things thin." He leveled his blue gaze on her. "How attached were you to Lord Burbridge?"

For the second time that day Brynnde found herself gaping. "Very," she finally managed. "I mean, as much as I could be under the circumstances. We suited," she declared, and realized she believed it to be true. She wondered if Garrick had felt the same.

Lord Averland nodded as if he'd suspected as much. "The two of you did seem to get on from the start. Damn shame about... Well, that's neither here nor there. Or it's there, at least, and not here. And here is all I'm concerned with." He smiled apologetically. "I'm rambling. Becoming an old man. Which is why I would so like to see you and your sister settled. Nicolas too, for that matter."

Nicolas! The thought sprang through Brynnde's mind. In all her selfish musings, she had forgotten Julia's *tendre* for Nicolas. And Brynnde was fairly certain Nicolas had not been entirely indifferent to Julia either. A desire to seek her brother out and suss the truth spurred Brynnde to her feet.

Her father looked up, surprised. "Yes, I suppose we're done," he said, only to be startled again when Brynnde swept in to kiss his cheek. "Christmas," he reminded her. "At the latest."

Brynnde hardly heard him in her rush to find her brother. Nicolas sat across from their mother at the card table, smiling indulgently as they played whist. Tessa, meanwhile, scowled irritably at Violet, who fumbled with her cards. Brynnde suspected only Maman would be sorry to have the game broken up.

"Nicolas," Brynnde said as she approached the table, "Papa wants a word with you."

"You can take his hand then," Maman instructed, but Brynnde smiled.

"Sorry, Maman, but he still has need of me as well."

Ignoring the curiosity on her mother's face, Brynnde hurried to catch up to Nicolas as he crossed the entry. "Is he still in the dining room?" he asked.

"No, I don't know," Brynnde said, causing Nicolas to raise an eyebrow. "Papa doesn't really—" Remembering her mother's obvious interest, she took her brother's arm and steered him toward the library in case Papa really was still in the dining room. "I have to ask you something."

"All right," said Nicolas, "though I can't imagine what you need to ask that you can't in front of—" His words stopped short and the amusement left his face. "If it's about Graeme Sommerford—"

"No," Brynnde said, "not him. But what about Julia?"

"Julia?"

"Sommerford," said Brynnde, her spirits sinking. Perhaps Nicolas had been more uninterested in her friend than she'd hoped.

"What of her?" Nicolas asked. The right corner of his mouth twitched, and Brynnde gasped.

"You *do* like her!"

"Like her? I suppose."

"Your mouth only twitches like that when you're afraid you've been found out in something," Brynnde accused. "Like the time Papa asked about Jasper, and you thought he'd discovered you were the one to leave his stall open."

Nicolas sighed. "So?"

"So," Brynnde echoed.

Nicolas shrugged. "I hardly had the opportunity to get to know her, and there's no chance of it now. So why are you asking?"

"There must be a way," Brynnde muttered. "She likes you, too, you see. What she knows of you, anyway," Brynnde added. "Too much time with you and you might yet put her off."

"Well, she'll have to go on liking me then," said Nicolas, "since we will not be spending any time together."

"We can't invite them here," Brynnde went on, half to herself, "and they won't invite us there, either, but there must be *somewhere* we can both get invited."

"They won't be going anywhere in society until they clear up Graeme's mess," said Nicolas.

"They can leave him home," Brynnde said dismissively, her mind working furiously. "It isn't fair to—oh! I have it!"

"I hope it isn't catching," said Nicolas.

Brynnde spared him a scowl. "We'll get invited to the Crabbages'. Violet will have me and the Sommerford sisters as guests and—"

"Sir Everett would never," Nicolas told her. "Too expensive."

"But Lady Crabbage would, if only to get the gossip first hand," said Brynnde. "She could hardly pass up the chance to be able to say she had the Sommerford daughters under her roof!"

"All well and good," said Nicolas, "but I don't see how you going to the Crabbages' gets me any time with Julia Sommerford."

"You will come after a few days to fetch me home. Some emergency."

"And? If I arrive only to leave again with you, I still won't have spent any time in the company of Lady Julia."

"I'll be too sick or something to go. You'll have to stay until I'm better."

"I always thought of Tessa as the diabolical one," Nicolas said, "but you're causing me to reconsider."

"I'm sure Violet will be happy to take me back to Lowlea with her," said Brynnde, warm now with inspiration.

"And is she friendly enough with the Sommerfords to ask them?" Nicolas inquired.

"They met while here, so at least there is an established acquaintance," Brynnde mused. She gnawed her lip. "I will slip a note in as well," she decided. "They will be sure to come if they know I'm there."

"Bryn..." Nicolas warned, but she waved away his caution.

"It is the best possible scheme. You'll see. I'll begin to feel low, so low that Violet will become anxious and do anything to enliven my spirit. Then I'll tell her I need to get away from here." Brynnde thought of Mr. Dallweather and knew she could leverage him as an excuse for wanting to put some distance between herself and Aux Arbres. "She'll be prompted to suggest we go to Lowlea, and the plan will be in motion." She gave a sharp nod of satisfaction.

Nicolas sighed. "Well, I'm not going to stop you," was all he said.

"But you'll come when I send for you?" Brynnde asked.

"If only to see the mess you make of things," her brother told her with a smile. "It will certainly be worth the trip."

13

———

*P*utting her plan in motion proved more difficult than Brynnde expected thanks to Mr. Dallweather.

Violet and horses were not on friendly terms, so Brynnde left off her usual rides and agreed to walk with her friend instead. She did not count on Mr. Dallweather also getting his exercise in that way.

She and Violet were strolling along the worn path that bordered the chase on the eastern side of Aux Arbres when they encountered him coming very jauntily in their direction. For a harebrained moment Brynnde considered diving into the trees, but of course she could not, and it was too late besides—Mr. Dallweather had spotted them and lengthened his stride so as to reach them.

Beside her, Violet went wide-eyed and still as a deer, and the errant thought that at least hunting season had not yet begun sailed through Brynnde's mind. Not that Mr. Dallweather hunted, a point in his favor. Then Mr. Dallweather stood before them, tall and paunchy and more salt than pepper on his head when he removed his hat and bowed to them. He wore a coat of questionable carmine color.

"Miss Archambault, Miss... Crabbage, was it?" Violet nodded. "Would you allow me to walk with you?"

Brynnde nearly rocked back on her heels at his forwardness. Very unlike the Mr. Dallweather she knew. "We are going in two opposite directions," she pointed out.

"I do not mind turning around," he told her with a smile, and he did so, then stuck out his elbows like a deranged chicken so that each lady might take one.

Violet looked behind his back to Brynnde, her mouth agape. Brynnde only shrugged and accepted the arm.

"Well, this makes my day much more pleasant," said Mr. Dallweather.

And ours far less so, thought Brynnde, then immediately felt guilty. He was not a bad man. Kind, and respectable, and though Belle Weather was not nearly as grand as Aux Arbres, it was a fine enough house.

"Where are you ladies off to this morning?" Mr. Dallweather quizzed.

"Nowhere in particular," Brynnde told him. "Violet isn't fond of riding, so we thought we'd walk and enjoy the last of the good weather."

Mr. Dallweather nodded. "I also am not fond of horses and find I do much better on foot." He went on to ask Violet about her family and Lowlea, and soon Brynnde found herself eclipsed from the conversation while Violet and Mr. Dallweather deepened their acquaintance. How good of Violet to take on the task of sparing her from unwanted advances, Brynnde thought, by occupying Mr. Dallweather so. She made a mental note to walk in a different direction on the morrow.

Brynnde was pulled from her musings by the realization

they had come to Belle Weather. "Do come in for some refreshment," Mr. Dallweather entreated, but when Brynnde opened her mouth to decline, something astounding happened: Violet accepted.

Snapping her mouth closed, Brynnde looked closely at Violet, noting her flushed cheeks and shining eyes. Not all from the exercise and fresh air, Brynnde suspected. Violet turned to Brynnde as they followed Mr. Dallweather inside, her smile a mixture of delight and apology. "I hope you don't mind?"

What could Brynnde say? "Of course not. I could do with some tea, but—"

A cacophony of hounds overrode her remaining words —"watch out for the dogs."

She grimaced as half a dozen Irish setters beset them, but Violet only laughed and bent to pet each in turn. Mr. Dallweather whistled for the dogs and they obediently departed, moving to lie around the sitting room fire. "I am so sorry," Mr. Dallweather fretted. "I should have warned you, or put them away before inviting you in, or—"

"No harm done," Violet assured him with another laugh.

Brynnde wondered at this new aspect of her usually shy friend. And then another thought washed over her. If Violet became attached to Mr. Dallweather, how would Brynnde ever get her back to Lowlea? Her entire plan hinged on that.

She had to act.

Brynnde did not possess Tessa's ability to shed tears whenever it suited her purpose. She would have to make do with her best pout. She endeavored to imagine something that would truly put her out—Parnassus ill, perhaps? Or this very situation of being obliged to spend time at Belle Weather and needing to extract her friend. That was upsetting enough.

It worked. Violet's smile faded at the sight of Brynnde's furrowed brow and downcast eyes. A stab of regret pierced Brynnde's heart—she hated to think she was dampening Violet's happiness—but unbeknownst to Brynnde the guilt only added to her morose expression.

"Brynnde?" Violet asked, "Are you unwell?"

Mr. Dallweather hopped to in his helpful way. "I will call for tea directly," he said and swiftly left the room in search of his housekeeper who, Brynnde knew from having been told many times over, was half deaf and never heard the bell.

"I am only sad," Brynnde said once their host had gone. "I have these moments…" She realized with a start that it was not a lie. Over the handful of weeks since coming home to Aux Arbres, Brynnde often found her mind wandering toward what might have been had her engagement held. She could not account for the sorrow those thoughts gave her except that she had lost people of which she'd become quite fond.

"Oh, and how thoughtless of me to insist on coming here!" cried Violet. She reached over and grasped Brynnde's hands in her own. "After you told me you wish to avoid becoming its mistress!"

Brynnde wanted to say Belle Weather gave her no particular grief, but in order for her plan to play out, she knew she must grasp the line Violet had thrown her. "Yes, well, it does distress me a bit," she hedged, hating to lie outright. And the idea of becoming Mrs. Dallweather *did* distress her.

"I will make sure we do not stay long," Violet promised.

Just then Mr. Dallweather arrived with the tea tray, his elderly housekeeper following in his wake. "It is easier for me to carry it," he explained. "Poor old Betty has difficulty holding it steady." He set the tray down on the table and waved Betty away when she moved in to pour. "We'll take care of it, thank you, Betty!" he all but shouted. Betty cocked a thick eyebrow at him, looking at him as if he'd gone mad, then scuttled out of the room.

"Oh, do let me," said Violet when Mr. Dallweather moved to pour the tea. She took the teapot and did a very pretty job of serving, Brynnde thought. Again Brynnde wondered at her friend's sudden sociability. Then again, Mr. Dallweather was far from an intimidating presence. Brynnde could not be surprised that Violet was at ease around him.

Brynnde sipped at her tea, nibbled sponge cake, and assured Violet and their host she was well, only fatigued. She half listened to them chatter about London—Mr. Dallweather did possess a small residence there but only went on business or for new books, which of course delighted Violet. Still, Brynnde was aware of Violet's occasional glances to check on her and tried to smile in just the right semi-sad kind of way but had no clue whether she hit the mark. Acting was so much more Tessa's skill.

Once they finished with the tea, Violet sprang from her seat. "I am sorry," she said breathlessly as both Brynnde and Mr. Dallweather rose. She looked over at Brynnde, fresh worry lighting her eyes. "We do really appreciate your hospitality, Mr. Dallweather, but I fear Miss Archambault is putting on a brave face, and I think it best to get her home."

"Certainly, certainly!" said Mr. Dallweather. "If you give me but a moment, I'll escort you." He glanced around as though expecting Betty to appear, but all the sudden energy in the room only served to work up the dogs. They uncurled from their places beside the fire and came to sniff at Brynnde and Violet's skirts, one or two of them even reaching to snuffle available hands.

"Oh, I am sorry!" Mr. Dallweather stammered. "Ivy, Clancy, Baron, Daisy, Dane, Flann!" At the sound of its name, each dog dropped obediently to a sitting position.

"We won't inconvenience you any longer," Violet insisted. "We would feel awful were you to catch something on our account." She looked again to Brynnde, clearly searching for support.

Brynnde knew Mr. Dallweather possessed a particular fear of illness. She supposed his wife's early death might have something to do with it, and felt another prick of guilt for using it against him. But dire circumstances called for strict measures. Brynnde turned her head and coughed into her glove.

Mr. Dallweather's eyes widened and he began to usher the ladies out of the room and toward the entry. "Well, if you're certain..." He flexed his hands in obvious agitation. "I hate to think, were you to need help... To be on your own..."

"It isn't so far a walk, Mr. Dallweather," said Brynnde. "And we are both quite refreshed thanks to your tea."

Mr. Dallweather nodded. "Yes, well, if you're sure..." he said again, holding open the door. Their last sight of him was of his discreetly bringing a handkerchief to his nose and mouth while his dogs milled at his feet.

14

"You aren't really ill?" Violet asked once they'd lost sight of Belle Weather.

"Not of body," Brynnde assured. She glanced up at the sky where gray clouds had begun to gather. "We should hurry back in case it rains, else we might both catch ill after all."

They put all their energy into walking, hardly speaking until they reached Aux Arbres. As they rounded the house and the first droplets made themselves known, Violet voiced the very thought Brynnde had aimed to plant. "It must be difficult, with Mr. Dallweather constantly at hand."

Brynnde saw how Violet chewed her lip and reached over to squeeze her friend's hand. "Yes." Then, taking a cue from Tessa's theatrics, she heaved a sigh.

"What is it?" Violet asked. "Oh, no, that is such a stupid question," she added, then went on, "What can I do to help?"

They achieved the entry hall and before Brynnde could answer Violet's question Lady Averland sailed out of the drawing room. "Girls! Where in heavens have you been?

The storm was coming on—I watched it from the windows and could only worry you would be caught in the torrent!" She turned to Violet. "Your mother would drop me in an instant were I to allow you to fall ill while you are here!"

"We are fine, Maman," Brynnde said. "Home just in time." As if on cue, a spate of rain tapped the windows.

"And missed tea," Lady Averland sniffed as the girls trailed her back to the drawing room.

"We came across Mr. Dallweather on our walk," Brynnde informed her, striving to keep her tone light, "and took tea with him."

Lady Averland stopped short so that Brynnde and Violet nearly ran up the back of her. She turned slowly to peer at Brynnde over her shoulder. Then her eyes tracked over to Violet. Each of the girls held her breath and waited.

Abruptly, Lady Averland turned away and once again began her forward march. "Well, then," was all she said. The girls exchanged uncertain glances before following, drawn on—at least in Brynnde's mind—by a kind of dread as well as mere force of her mother's bulk, which had a way of pulling things along in its wake. They'd long since given up keeping good china on tables at hip height.

In the drawing room, Lady Averland arranged herself on one sofa, and as she took up most of the space there, Brynnde and Violet settled on another. "We're so sorry to delay your tea," Violet ventured.

"Oh, hardly," Lady Averland replied with a wave. "Why should I have waited? Who knew when you would be home?"

Brynnde had to purse her lips to keep from smiling.

"How did you find Mr. Dallweather?" her mother asked.

Violet answered before Brynnde could. "Walking."

Brynnde resorted to biting the insides of her cheeks. She

would *not* smile. "I believe Maman meant to ask whether he was well."

"Oh." Violet blushed and ducked her head.

"He was," Brynnde told her mother. "Well, that is."

Lady Averland's eyes remained on Violet.

"And, as we said, kind enough to invite us for tea after our long walk," Brynnde went on.

"Only to release you into the storm," sniffed Lady Averland. "Not even the decency to see you home."

Violet's head snapped up. "Oh, but he would have! He wanted to!" She looked to Brynnde for support. "We told him not to bother himself."

Brynnde nodded. "Yes, we knew we could make it home before the rain, and there was no sense in poor Mr. Dallweather having to trudge home in it."

Lady Averland's eyes shifted between the two girls. "You are awfully keen to clothe him in virtue," she remarked. "But if he is to be a member of the family one day, I suppose you'd best get in the habit now."

Brynnde's mouth fell open and Violet ducked her head again.

"Nothing is settled, of course," Lady Averland continued. "Nothing announced. But really, Brynnde, I don't know why you put it off. It is by far the best settlement you could hope for.

"Your father says to give you time. For what, I wonder? No sense mourning what you almost had. Such a freak occurrence, that. You won't have another son of an earl turning up at your feet. You must make the most of your opportunities, small as they may be."

Brynnde understood something then. Her mother's world had been tilted off axis when Brynnde had landed such a prize fiancé. Now that the engagement had fallen off,

Lady Averland's worldview turned upright again. Tessa would get another Season, but Brynnde was expected to accept whatever, and whomever, was placed in front of her.

Her mother watched her narrowly. Brynnde focused on her hands in her laps and willed them not to fidget.

"We could have saved so much money and trouble if you'd accepted Dallweather before the Season," said Lady Averland. "We would not have needed to exit so early, and Tessa would have had time to select a suitor."

Select a suitor? As if they'd been offered to her like tea sandwiches on a platter? So far as Brynnde remembered, the gentlemen who'd lined up early in the Season to get fair Tessa's attention abandoned her almost as quickly after tasting some of her venom. Few were willing to put up with Tessa's haughtiness, especially not the wealthy, titled men who had a slew of more appealing options.

"Lord Marchand was, I believe, very close to making an offer," Lady Averland said, "And Lord Caddow as well."

Brynnde had no choice but to nod at her hands repentantly. She longed to shout that the engagement's dissolution had not been her fault, and that Lords Marchand and Caddow had neither looked at Tessa more than twice, but to what end? Her mother would only see her arguing as proof of her unworthiness for anything better than Mr. Dallweather.

And maybe she was unworthy, even of him. How much easier life would be if Brynnde could simply agree to do what everyone wanted! They would all be happy then. All but her, anyway.

The rustling of her mother's skirts caused Brynnde to look up. Lady Averland rose from her couch. "I am going to go lie down before dinner. The rain always brings me headache." She swished out of the room.

After the sound of Lady Averland's footsteps faded, Violet looked up and met Brynnde's gaze. "Will you? Accept Mr. Dallweather?"

Brynnde sighed. "I would rather not."

"He seems like such a nice man," said Violet.

"He *is* nice. Almost too nice for me." Brynnde tilted her head as she considered. "He has few faults of character," she admitted, "aside from an excessive love of dogs, and a dislike of horses. And he is so *old*." She shook her head. "I cannot see him as anything but a kind of uncle. I would much rather live out my days here, a spinster, than as Mrs. Dallweather."

"I do not mind older men," Violet said quietly. "They are so much more settled than the younger ones. So steady. And I like dogs," she added.

Brynnde regarded her friend with new perspective. "Violet! I do believe you have formed a fast attachment to my suitor!"

Violet's cheeks and ears turned a vivid pink. "No! I—"

Brynnde waved off her discomfort. "You won't get any contest from me over it. But Maman might see it as an affront. In fact," Brynnde mused, liking the idea more and more, "You would surely make him happier than I. The two of you suit, I think. And we would be neighbors!"

A light of hope dawned in Violet's cognac-colored eyes. Then dimmed almost as quickly. "But Mr. Dallweather's interest is in you," she said.

"Only because he hadn't met you before," Brynnde told her. "I am sure, after that tea, his head must be spinning with thoughts of you. The way the two of you chattered on like old friends..." A memory of comfortable conversation between herself and Garrick arose like a menacing spirit and threw Brynnde off track. How easy he had been to talk to!

Violet reached over and squeezed Brynnde's hand, just as she had done at Belle Weather. "There, I've done it again. Made you sad by forcing you to think about your situation."

"I cannot escape it," said Brynnde. "Not here, when it is all around me. I cannot go back to London because that will only remind me all the more. And here, Mr. Dallweather is always under foot." It was almost Tessa worthy, Brynnde thought. She bowed her head over her lap and peeked at Violet from under her lashes, willing her friend to come to the solution.

Violet stared at the far wall of the parlour for what felt like an inordinate amount of time. Then she gasped. "Oh! But what if you were to come to Lowlea?"

Brynnde raised her head and put on her best thinking expression. "Well, it *would* allow me some respite... Would your mother and father permit it?"

"Oh, I'm sure they would be delighted!" said Violet, and Brynnde recalled that her friend was ever blind to her parents' faults, namely her father's dislike of company as an expense.

"And do you think...?" Brynnde began, "It would make me feel ever so much better if—if Julia and Eleanor might be invited, too."

Violet blinked owlishly. "The Sommerfords?"

"I didn't get to say a proper goodbye, you see." This time Brynnde did not have to pretend; her sorrow surprised her by climbing her throat and making her words thick. "We were going to be sisters."

Violet squeezed Brynnde's hand yet again. "I don't know them very well, but we can certainly extend an invitation. Will *your* parents allow you to come for a visit?"

"I will make sure of it," Brynnde resolved. "Oh, thank you, Violet! I feel so much more cheerful at the notion of going away for a while!" And with mild astonishment, Brynnde realized it was true. She felt as though a stone, so long lodged in her chest she'd grown accustomed to the weight, had been lifted, leaving her freer to breathe properly.

Violet, on the other hand, appeared a little melancholy about the plan. Brynnde could see the way her friend tried to smile, yet there was moistness in her eyes. "What is it?" Brynnde asked. "You think perhaps your parents will not allow so many visitors?"

"Oh, no, Mama always tells me I should have more friends," said Violet. "I was only thinking, if we go away so soon, I will have no opportunity to—to become better acquainted with Mr. Dallweather."

Brynnde could not but concede the point. After all, what prize was there for Violet in this scheme? A good, sweet friend like Violet would help in any case, but Brynnde wanted to reward her. And if Mr. Dallweather was Violet's choice of trophy, well, she was welcome to him.

Brynnde chewed her lip as she contemplated, then brightened. "You will come back with me after the visit. And spend more time here, in the vicinity of Mr. Dallweather."

Violet nodded, though Brynnde saw the answer did not entirely please her. Not having known the agony of being parted from someone who ignited passion in her, Brynnde could not comprehend Violet's reluctance.

"And we needn't be gone long," Violet said as though cheering herself with the words. Then she hesitated and eyed Brynnde uncertainly. "Need we?"

"I don't know," Brynnde admitted. "How long does it take to mend a wounded heart, do you think?" When Violet only blinked, Brynnde went on, "Well, the sooner gone the sooner returned. We'll post letters to your mother and the Sommerfords this afternoon and plan to leave morning after next."

There. Done. Brynnde went up to dress for dinner feeling very efficient indeed.

15

———

The day before they departed for Lowlea, Mr. Dallweather sent around a note to check they'd made it home and that Brynnde's health was improving. "Isn't that kind of him!" Violet said, rather more often than necessary to Brynnde's way of thinking. Her mother agreed, equally repeatedly and with pointed looks in Brynnde's direction, that Mr. Dallweather showed great strength of character. Tessa only smirked.

Brynnde was quite happy to escape.

She had visited Lowlea once as a young girl, but in the eyes of a nineteen-year-old it appeared vastly different. Instead of just another big house, Brynnde immediately noted how small it was compared to Aux Arbres, and how shabby. Older than Aux Arbres, the stones at the corners had begun to crumble and some roof shingles were missing. And though some attempt had been made to keep the lawns in order, the result was uneven at best. Patches of dead brown grass dotted the green. In front of the house, an elaborate fountain featuring an angel taking flight from what appeared to be a mountaintop was choked with ivy, and the standing water in the basin gave off a musty smell.

Despite the disrepair, however, Lowlea exuded warmth in the person of Lady Crabbage, who greeted them with bearlike hugs as they descended the coach. "Poor girl," she said to Brynnde, and flicked away a tear Brynnde was sure wasn't there, "of course you must get away for a space! Here there will be nothing to trouble you."

As if in answer—and direct refute—Oliver came barreling out of the house. "What are you doing here?" he demanded as he halted before his sister. "We only just got rid of you!"

To Brynnde's astonishment, Violet only smiled and said sweetly, "I think I hear Master Collins calling for you." At which point Oliver took to his heels and darted away around the corner of the house. When she caught Brynnde's wide-eyed stare, Violet lifted one shoulder and said, "It's the one certain way to get him to go away, threaten him with his tutor."

It was a side of Violet Brynnde had never suspected existed.

While Lady Crabbage issued curt instructions for the luggage, Violet and Brynnde drifted indoors to refresh themselves. Violet waved the maid away and showed Brynnde to the guest room, which was much larger than Brynnde's room at home, but again showed signs of age: a rug worn almost through in places, fraying bedclothes, faded curtains, and wrinkling wallpaper. A dampness hung in the air that Brynnde attributed to the old stone weeping beneath the plaster. The only place the original stone remained visible was around the fireplace.

She took a seat on the bed, testing the mattress, and was gratified to find it comfortable. She lay down to be sure.

Next thing she knew, there came a knock and the door opened. Molly entered with Brynnde's trunk in tow.

"Sleeping?" Molly asked as Brynnde struggled to sit up. The mattress was comfortable, yes, but sagged just enough in the middle to trap a person.

"What time is it?" Brynnde asked.

"Time to get out of those travel clothes and dressed for dinner," said Molly. She took Brynnde's wrists and heaved her upright. Brynnde slid off the side of the bed and allowed Molly to help her with her clothes. She just finished pinning up her hair as the dinner bell rang.

"What do you make of their kitchen?" Brynnde asked as she slipped on her shoes.

Molly wrinkled her nose. "Well, it's no Aux Arbres. They're a nice enough lot, but nervous like." She shook her head in wonder. "I got out from under foot quick as I could. The cook runs it like the army from what I can tell."

Brynnde thought it not out of the question that Sir Everret might have hired an army cook. Worse, a soldier who didn't know how to cook at all. She went down to dinner with little enthusiasm.

She needn't have worried. The food was, if not grand, palatable and filling. Lady Crabbage did most of the talking, naturally, unabated by her husband, who devoted himself to eating. Violet also remained mostly quiet, and Brynnde wondered whether the meals were like that even without visitors—Lady Crabbage filling the vast dining room with her words. She was a babbling brook and everyone else mere rocks over which she washed herself.

The thought made Brynnde want to laugh, and she had to place her napkin to her mouth to hold it in. Lady Crabbage took this move exactly for its opposite and ceased her prattle to croon instead. "Oh, my dear," she said with a sympathetic look at her guest, "I know this must be such a trying time for you. Why, your wedding would have been this month! And now..." She shook her head over the tragedy. "Be sure that I am here if you need to talk about anything."

Violet threw Brynnde a wholly unnecessary apprehensive look, for Brynnde knew better than to tell Lady Crabbage anything she did not want to hear coming back to her via a multitude of whispers. And she'd had her fill of those in London.

Amusement thus smothered, Brynnde lowered her napkin and attempted to appear suitably morose. "Thank you, Lady Crabbage. I believe the lovely scenery here at Lowlea will be sufficient to cheer me."

This pronouncement garnered Sir Everret's attention and approval. For the first time that evening he looked up from his meal. He beamed at Brynnde and said, "Quite." Then he returned to his slightly overcooked mutton.

"Oh!" yelped Lady Crabbage then, causing everyone at the table to jump. Sir Everret's gravy went flying, but his wife took no notice. "The Sommerford girls have written you, Violet. I meant to give you the letter earlier but then you each were resting. Remind me, and I'll give it you after dinner." She wriggled in her seat like a giddy schoolgirl or, Brynnde thought, perhaps more like a fat hen settling on her eggs. The napkin returned to Brynnde's mouth.

Again, Lady Crabbage took it as a sign. "Should I not have mentioned them? Of course I shouldn't have! Oh, Brynnde, do please forgive me! I should have given Violet the letter in private. They are assuredly the last people you want to hear about, the last name you want to hear uttered—"

"It's all right, Mama," Violet said. "Brynnde and Julia and Eleanor have no ill feelings between them."

"Actually," Brynnde added, "I miss them terribly. We had become very good friends."

Lady Crabbage changed direction without misstep. "And so of course you're so sad to hear their names spoken aloud! I am sorry, my dear, really I am. I've only added to your sorrow."

"I've invited them to visit," Violet went on. Brynnde marveled at her friend's patience but supposed it came from a lifetime of practice.

"It would very much delight me to see them," said Brynnde, "if it doesn't trouble you too much to have them." She imitated Tessa's wide-eyed, plaintive look, the one that Papa could not resist.

"Of course not!" crowed Lady Crabbage, and this time Sir Everret's knife went wide. He sighed and persevered, not allowing his wife nor his meat to best him, for which Brynnde silently applauded him. Lady Crabbage's eyes, meanwhile, had taken on a brilliance akin to religious fervor, and Brynnde knew they'd won. Lady Crabbage could not resist having the daughters of an earl under her roof; any protest by Sir Everret would fall on stale ground. Not that he seemed inclined to argue.

Brynnde wished the rest of the dinner toward a speedy end, eager to adjourn and hear the letter from Julia and Eleanor. She had included a note of her own in Violet's missive and hoped the sisters had answered her directly.

When Sir Everret finally sat back in his chair, his appetite seemingly satisfied, he smiled at each of the ladies in turn. "Now, then," he said, "what would you like to talk about?"

Brynnde thought she would jump out of her seat from

the anticipation. She clutched the arms of her chair to hold herself in it.

Sir Everret's eyes crinkled with amusement. "No, no, I know," he chuckled. "And I'd just as soon enjoy my pipe in peace. So—" He made a shooing motion with his hands.

Lady Crabbage rose, and Violet and Brynnde shot to their feet as well, in a fashion bordering on unladylike.

"I do believe you'll be glad when Oliver can attend you," declared Lady Crabbage to her husband.

Sir Everret grunted. "I'll store up my peace and quiet in the meantime."

Brynnde thought Oliver could hardly be any more talkative than his mother. Then again, she would not be keen to find out. She eagerly followed Lady Crabbage and Violet out of the dining room, very nearly treading on their hems in her haste.

In the parlour, Lady Crabbage hefted her bulk into an oversized chair. Violet and Brynnde remained standing, expectant. Lady Crabbage peered up at them, clearly put out. "What is it, girls?"

"The letter, Mama?" Violet asked.

"Oh, of course, of course," said Lady Crabbage. She gestured at the spindle-legged writing desk situated against the far wall of the room. "It's in there."

Violet dutifully went to the desk while Brynnde did all she could not to bounce on her toes like a little girl awaiting a sweet.

"I don't—" Violet began, then said, "Oh, here it is."

Brynnde would have opened it then and there, but Violet strolled back to the sofa and settled herself, holding the letter by the edges as though it were something holy. Or dirty. She looked up, and Brynnde realized she was hovering. So with a deep breath, Brynnde seated herself beside her friend.

Violet regarded the direction on the letter. "Lovely handwriting," she remarked.

Brynnde thought she might burst. "Probably Eleanor's," she said, pleased with how even her voice remained.

Violet nodded and flipped the letter over, pausing again over the wax seal that depicted the Earl of Darley's coat of arms: a greyhound surrounded by acanthus leaves. Brynnde wanted to howl, was sure she would if Violet opined on the seal, but Violet merely broke it and opened the letter.

Brynnde saw at once the handwriting inside differed from the direction on the front. The scrawl and blotches were surely indicative of Julia's energy. Violet began skimming, but Lady Crabbage demanded, "Well? Read it, then." So Violet did.

" 'Dear Miss Crabbage, Thank you so much for your recent invitation to Lowlea. I regret—' "

Brynnde's breath halted in her chest.

Violet continued, oblivious to her friend's discomfort, " 'my sister Eleanor cannot come with me, but I do gladly accept. It will be most pleasant to be away from home for a few days, and especially to see Miss Archambault if she is there. I do hope she is, otherwise would you be so kind as to forward the enclosed note to her?' "

Here Violet fumbled the page and a second folded page fell out from behind it, having been slipped between the two pages directed at Violet. It was sealed and had Brynnde's name on it. Violet handed it to her friend and summarized the remainder of the letter.

"It says she will come on Wednesday."

"Day after tomorrow!" cried Lady Crabbage. "We will have so much to do to be ready."

Brynnde couldn't imagine what needed to be done besides the making up of a room, but experience informed her that Lady Crabbage enjoyed a bit of drama wherever she could find—or inject—it.

She looked at the letter in her hand. "Are you going to open it?" Violet asked.

Brynnde wanted to, badly, but feared Lady Crabbage would demand to hear it, too. "I'd much rather read a book," she said.

"Oh, good, you can read to me while I do my needlework," announced Lady Crabbage as she fished around in a wicker basket beside her chair. "Violet reads so monotonously it puts me to sleep."

Violet flushed and ducked her head. Brynnde felt bad for her but could not think of a ready defense. Instead she smiled wanly and took the book Violet handed over to her. She found the marked page and began to read, all the time aware of the sealed letter on her lap that seemed to burn through her skirts.

She read for she knew not how long, nor did she absorb any of the novel's plot. Then, at long last Lady Crabbage yawned in such a loud way as to interrupt Brynnde's flow of words. "You do read quite well, my dear," Lady Crabbage said, "but I believe I must retire now." She waggled a finger at the girls. "No reading on without me!"

She rose and the girls did as well. "Don't stay up too late," Lady Crabbage admonished as she sailed out of the room.

Violet tipped a knowing look at Brynnde. "Mama sleeps later than anyone else but likes to pretend she's the first one up every morning."

Brynnde smiled, but it turned into a yawn of her own

that she strove to hide behind her hand. "I am sorry. Even with the rest after our trip—"

"Oh, I know," assured Violet. "I am likewise fatigued. Shall we go up?"

Once safely in her room, Brynnde could wait no longer. Despite exhaustion, she threw herself onto her bed and tore open the seal on her letter. What she found astounded her. A note in Julia's trademark scrawl, yes, but also another, smaller card.

Brynnde skimmed Julia's note first. The usual pleasantries about being so glad to see Brynnde again, not being able to wait to tell her everything that had gone on, then an apology for bothering her with the unsolicited enclosure. " 'Garrick felt the need to—' "

Brynnde didn't read the rest of the sentence, instead hurrying to break the seal on the final card. She wasn't sure what she expected or hoped for, but just the sight of Garrick's strong, confident handwriting seized Brynnde's heart.

Dear Miss Archambault,

Allow me to say again how sorry I am for all that happened. Though neither you nor I are to blame, we are, I believe, the chief sufferers of these events. I do hope, in time, we will be able to resume our former friendliness.

Yours,

Burbridge

FORMER FRIENDLINESS? Brynnde wanted to spit like an angry cat. It failed to occur to her that she'd hoped for just the same friendliness only minutes before. Somehow, having it put plainly on paper by the man she'd meant to marry felt like—like—she didn't know what, but not good. It was so formal, so stiff, with no real feeling behind it. He might have said he hoped they'd see each other in London again some day. It meant, at the end of the day, that he would not seek her out.

It was so... final.

Until that moment, Brynnde had not realized she'd still held hope in her heart for... Something. A reconciliation? A re-engagement? Some kind of attachment. No, she did not love Garrick, but a tiny part of her had hoped—believed— he loved her. She'd taken energy from that, and this note snatched it away.

Exhaustion fell heavily over Brynnde, and she slumped over the pages in her hand. Suddenly, the prospect of seeing Julia no longer filled her with joy but apprehension. What if Julia talked about him? Each mention would be like a fork tine to Brynnde's heart. She could not endure it.

On the other hand, it would make pretending to fall ill all the easier. Sick at heart was the worst kind of sick.

That was Brynnde's last coherent thought before morning.

16

Molly bustled in, and if she'd knocked, Brynnde had not heard. Instead, she awoke to Molly's clucking over her rumpled dress. "You should have rang for me," Molly chided.

"It was late," mumbled Brynnde, "I didn't want to disturb you."

"Well, and it's still that much work for me to get this dress tidied," said Molly as she unlaced her mistress.

"I'm sorry, Molly," Brynnde said as she washed up with the fresh water the maid had brought up.

Molly shook out the abused garment and a couple papers fluttered to the rug, having been caught in some lace. Molly stooped to retrieve them, but Brynnde swept across the room to get there first. "It's nothing," she said, "I only fell asleep reading."

The maid shrugged, though she regarded Brynnde with interest. "Not as if I could read them myself anyway." She returned her attention to the dress. "I only hope the ink didn't muss."

Once Brynnde was freshly clothed, Molly asked, "Did you want a tray, or were you going down to breakfast?"

Brynnde was sorely tempted to hide in her room and nurse her bruised pride but decided against it. Violet and Lady Crabbage both were likely to descend upon her if she did not appear. Also, Brynnde wanted to save their concern for her planned illness. Though she felt sick at heart already, quite capable of taking to her bed, she wanted time with Julia before succumbing to the ailment that would bring Nicolas to Lowlea.

"I'll go down," said Brynnde. She slid the letters into the pages of a book she'd brought and left it on the dressing table. "Was anyone else awake?"

"Only the staff as I saw," said Molly, "and that imp of a boy. He was out running around in the garden, if that's what it is."

Brynnde reasoned that Oliver had surely eaten up in his nursery or schoolroom or whatever he had; she could not expect him as company at breakfast, thank goodness. She made her way down and had just filled her plate from the overladen sideboard when Violet entered the dining room. They chatted pleasantly over breakfast and agreed it would be best to finish before Lady Crabbage arrived. Remarking the fine weather, they went out to walk in the garden.

Brynnde immediately understood Molly's comment. If the front lawns of Lowlea were patchy and its fountain untended, the rear lawns were overgrown and chaotic. Cobbled paths heaved up uneven from the ground and occasional holes promised rabbits or other rodents had taken up residence. Only sporadic spots of color could be seen through the tall greenery, and which plants were deliberate and which were weeds could not be readily discerned.

Violet ducked her head in embarrassment as Brynnde

stared around them as they walked. More than once Brynnde lost her footing over an irregular stone. She knew she should keep her eyes on the path, but there was too much to see. It was the most disarrayed garden she'd ever encountered.

"Papa cannot manage to keep gardeners," Violet explained so quietly Brynnde almost did not hear above the buzzing of insects in the tall grass. "The grounds are extensive and Papa prefers to maintain the house instead."

Brynnde comprehended Violet meant Sir Everret chose not to spend money on the grounds. Well, and if they never had visitors, why would he? Though the lack of pride in one's estate was alien to Brynnde's way of thinking. She loved Aux Arbres, and it would break her heart to see it in similar disrepair, outside or in.

"I do try to garden a bit," Violet went on. "But there's just so much of it."

Brynnde nodded and struggled for something to say. "It's rather wild," she mused. "Almost like something out of a fairy tale."

Violet smiled in a small, sad way. "Well, Oliver enjoys it at least. He hides from his tutor out here, and Master Collins has an aversion to insects, so it works quite well for him."

Brynnde could all too easily imagine Oliver catching bugs and bringing them into the schoolroom for Master Collins' appreciation.

They walked until they could no longer avoid returning to the house, each of them bracing for Lady Crabbage's overexcitement. They managed to get as far as the dining room unnoticed, were availing themselves of the cold collation laid out there, when Lady Crabbage burst in. "Oh, do hurry, girls! We have so much to do!"

"Like what, Mama?" Violet asked, and Brynnde could

only admire her serenity in the face of Lady Crabbage's energy.

"I've sent Isobel to air the room, but we need fresh flowers for the hall and the parlour."

Brynnde thought about the garden they'd just exited and couldn't fathom whence these flowers were to come.

Lady Crabbage stood before them, wringing her hands. "I suppose there's nothing to be done about the fountain, is there?" She looked plaintively at her daughter.

"I could ask Tom whether—" Violet began.

"Oh, how good of you! Tell him to drop all other work. If he can't get the fountain running, at least have him clean it up." More hand wringing. "Maybe she won't want to go into the back garden..." Lady Crabbage drifted out of the dining room, muttering to herself.

Violet grimaced across the table at Brynnde. "She is worried about the impression we will make."

Brynnde smiled. "Julia won't care," she said. "In fact, she'll probably count it an adventure."

"She seems very..." Violet's voice trailed as she sought the word she wanted. Giving up, she went on, "You became close while in London?"

"Oh, yes! During my—" But thinking of the engagement brought to mind the note from Garrick, and all Brynnde's joy fled like sunlight affronted by a cloud.

"Oh, Brynnde, I am sorry!" said Violet. "I shouldn't have... That is to say, are you certain you'll be all right to see her? It won't be too painful to you?"

"It's not Julia's fault. It's not even Lord Burbridge's fault. And I do not want to lose such a wonderful friendship just because one person had a terrible lapse in judgement."

Anyone else would have goggled for details, but Violet only nodded. Each having finished eating, they decided their best chance at redeemable flowers would be farther afield than Lowlea. "We'll stop to see Tom, then go on to see Mrs. Riffle. She has a lovely garden."

Tom turned out to be the eldest son of one of the tenants. Lady Crabbage had no claim on his work and no authority to demand he go fix the fountain, but Brynnde watched as Violet gently pleaded her case. Tom nodded along then shouted into the cottage behind him, "Goin' up ta the big house, Ma! Got some work needs doing!" He loped off without waiting for a response.

The girls watched him disappear. "He's a good sort, Tom," pronounced Violet. "I think he'd probably take care of our lawns, but Papa would never allow it."

Brynnde supposed Sir Everret would be too proud to accept that level of charity, or else afraid of what people might think when he didn't pay. "Well, and I'm sure Tom has work enough of his own," she remarked.

Violet nodded and they turned their steps farther down the lane. Once beyond the perimeter of the house, the land became lush and well tended. Picturesque. The contrast only served to further the impact of Lowlea's disrepair.

They walked a ways past many sweet little cottages until they arrived at one that Violet called Floribunda. The reason for the name was immediately clear. Huge flowers of every size and color sprang up around the house, and more still lined the post rail fence, reaching through and waving merrily, heavy flower heads bobbing.

"She certainly has enough to spare," said Brynnde.

Violet went to the door and knocked. It opened almost instantly, revealing the shortest woman Brynnde had ever seen. Many of the flowering plants were taller than she.

"Good morning, Mrs. Riffle!" said Violet a trifle too loudly.

Mrs. Riffle squinted up at Violet with beady, dark eyes. Her hair still held traces of the black it had once been, now mostly given over to gray, so that on the whole she reminded Brynnde of a shrewd pigeon. "Violet!" she said at length, as though it had taken her a moment to understand what she was seeing. "What brings you out this morning?"

Violet gestured back at Brynnde. "May I introduce my friend, Miss Archambault? She is visiting me for a few days."

The inkdrop eyes turned Brynnde's way. After a moment the woman nodded. "Come in, girls, come in." She stepped back into her cottage to make way for them.

Inside it was cozy, warm, and clean. Brynnde had not realized how chilled she'd become in the autumn air until the heat of the small space enveloped her. Mrs. Riffle bustled past them to usher them into a tiny sitting room where the girls sat nearly knee-to-knee with her.

"Tea?" Mrs. Riffle asked though already ensconced in a chair that dwarfed her.

"Oh, no, Mrs. Riffle," said Violet, still talking a bit more loudly than usual, though Brynnde saw no indication that Mrs. Riffle might be hard of hearing. "We only came to ask whether we might cut some of your lovely flowers?"

Mrs. Riffle's head bobbed, and Brynnde could not discern whether the woman meant it as her answer or whether she had some kind of palsy. But again, after a time Mrs. Riffle said, "Of course, dears. I do have plenty of them, don't I?" And she smiled in a way that told Brynnde the flowers were her pride and delight.

"They are the loveliest ones for miles," Violet agreed. "If we might just borrow some shears?"

The little woman slipped out of her chair and bobbled off. In her absence, Violet turned to Brynnde with a wan smile. "Mr. Riffle has been gone some fifteen years now, and her one son is fighting on the Peninsula. Papa lets her stay even though she can't afford to pay any rent. Other tenants take turns managing her bit of land and seeing she's fed. Poor old dear."

Brynnde strove to hide her surprise even as she was forced to revise her opinion of the notoriously miserly Sir Everret. Violet, however, appeared able to read Brynnde's thoughts. "Oh, I know what people think of Papa, maybe even say when none of us is within hearing. But if there is one thing he has taught me, it is that I have enough, more than enough really, and our time, effort, and money is better spent on those who do not than luxuries for ourselves. I am quite content with Lowlea, despite all its shortcomings. Why shouldn't Mrs. Riffle have a beautiful garden that brings her joy? Such a garden at Lowlea would only be taken for granted anyway. There," she said, plucking at her skirts, "I've said too much."

"No, not at all!" Brynnde exclaimed. "I admire your perspective, and it gives me a new point of view as well."

Violet turned faintly pink. "Well," she admitted, "if I did have a say, I would possibly hire a slightly better cook for Lowlea. Our meat is always too dry."

Brynnde laughed. "But she makes up for it with all the gravy."

Violet smiled. "Oh, yes, we never want for gravy!"

Mrs. Riffle returned then carrying garden shears and a pair of oversized gloves. "I only have the one pair, dearie," she said as she handed them to Violet.

"This will do," Violet told her. "Thank you, Mrs. Riffle."

The old woman followed them to the door. "The ones on the south side of the house are the prettiest," she advised.

The girls thanked her again and stepped around the

corner of the house. Violet made the first pass then handed the shears and gloves to Brynnde. Brynnde pulled the gloves over her own and wondered aloud at their size; they did not look like ordinary gardening gloves. To which Violet replied, "They're almost certainly Mr. Riffle's or their son's, I think."

The thought of poor, old Mrs. Riffle wearing her late husband's gloves while tending her garden put a tiny dent in Brynnde's heart. The bits of leather might be all she had left of him, or of her absent son. She felt compelled to move quickly so as to return the treasured items as soon as possible. Before long, she and Violet had amassed quite a pair of bouquets between them, almost too much to comfortably carry back to Lowlea. Juggling the stems, they somehow managed to knock at the cottage and return Mrs. Riffle's things, thanking her one last time before departing.

It required both Brynnde's hands to hold her share of the flowers, and the scent, though lovely, soon gave her a headache. Violet appeared similarly peaked, her eyes turning red around the rims, and she developed a small sniffle. Brynnde might have thought her friend was crying, but she'd seen these symptoms in Tessa and suspected they came from prolonged exposure to the heady blooms.

The flowers grew heavier with each step; by the time they reached Lowlea, Brynnde's arms ached. Lady Crabbage dashed out to meet them, somehow simultaneously praising the beauty of the flowers and scolding the girls for their long absence.

"Did Tom come see to the fountain?" Violet asked as she relinquished her colorful armload to her mother.

"Yes," said Lady Crabbage, and in the same breath, "Sally, bring me the vases for the hall and parlour!"

Within minutes a maid came scurrying with two large

vases. She set them on the hall table. "Oh, and a small one for Lady Julia's room," Lady Crabbage told her, and like a mouse on a mission the maid scampered off again.

"Here, now," Lady Crabbage said to Brynnde, whose arms remained filled with flowers, "help me arrange them, would you, dear?"

"Helping" turned out to mean moving flowers around under Lady Crabbage's direction. "That purple one," Lady Crabbage would say, "move it over by the yellow, and let's see how that looks." Lady Crabbage also reserved some of the best stems to be put in the smaller vase brought by Sally. All the while, Violet stood back with her handkerchief to her nose, her eyes red and rheumy.

At last it was done to Lady Crabbage's satisfaction, and as she took the second vase into the parlour and called to Sally to bring the small one to the guest room, Brynnde and Violet made their escape. They ventured out the front of the house to have a look at the cleaned fountain. To Brynnde's surprise and Violet's delight, it not only had been cleared of weeds but also flowed freely.

"Tom is very handy," said Violet. "More than a few times he's saved us some trouble."

And some money, Brynnde felt sure but did not say. Perhaps, as with Mrs. Riffle, Sir Everret showed his gratitude and generosity in other ways.

It astounded Brynnde, the difference the cleaned fountain made to the front of Lowlea. The patchy grass could easily be ascribed to the season, but having the fountain burbling made the house appear less like something abandoned, at least so long as one didn't look too closely at the places where the masonry gave way. "Maybe some ivy," Brynnde half mused.

"What?" Violet asked as they returned indoors.

"I was only thinking that having some ivy grow over the house might give it a distinguished look."

"Not in less than a day!" Violet laughed.

"Well, no," Brynnde agreed with a smile. "But over time, it might be a nice addition."

Violet appeared skeptical but did not refute the suggestion as they walked upstairs to refresh themselves and rest before the evening meal.

17

———

$\mathcal{J}$ulia arrived mid-morning the next day, Ridgemow being closer to Lowlea than Aux Arbres. She greeted Violet warmly, thanking her for the invitation, then squealed with delight at the sight of Brynnde and threw her arms around Brynnde's neck. "I didn't mention to Mama you'd be here, of course," Julia said as she released her friend. "She might not have let me come."

"But she might *have*," Brynnde said.

Julia shrugged and grinned. "Better to ask forgiveness later, though I doubt Mama would be truly angry. She was very fond of you."

The past tense barbed Brynnde's heart and called to mind Garrick's note.

Julia gave Brynnde's had a squeeze. "And still is," she assured. "At a distance. We all know it is not your fault. Oh, wait until I tell you—!"

Lady Crabbage darted out of the house at that moment, decrying that no one had summoned her to greet her guest.

"I am so sorry, Lady Julia!" she said, taking Julia's hand and leading her indoors, and calling unnecessary instructions over her shoulder as a footman brought in the luggage. Brynnde and Violet trailed after. "I do hope you'll enjoy your stay at Lowlea," she finished as they reached the parlour.

Julia's eyes travelled the room then lifted to view the ceiling as though unconvinced it might not fall in on her. "It's charming."

"Refreshment?" Lady Crabbage asked, steering Julia toward a sofa.

Julia gently disengaged herself from Lady Crabbage's hold. "I would much rather freshen up first. It isn't so long a journey, but..."

"Of course, my dear! I'll show you up—"

"We'll do it, Mama," inserted Violet. "So that you can see to tea."

They left Lady Crabbage muttering to herself about tea and hurried upstairs to closet themselves in Brynnde's room while Julia's trafficked with luggage and her maid. Julia bounced onto the bed while Violet chose a chair by the fireplace and Brynnde took the seat at the dressing table.

"So here is what happened," Julia began without preamble.

"We know Graeme is to marry Lady Elisabeth Talmidge," said Brynnde, "but when? And is her family furious?"

"Honora won't stop crying, but the rest of them are making the best of it, and in truth Elisabeth and Graeme are ridiculously happy, much more than they deserve to be under the circumstances," Julia added with a sniff. "After ruining it for everyone else."

Had they? Brynnde wondered. Perhaps Garrick felt he'd made an escape. He'd seemed genuinely angry that day in the townhouse garden, but that may have had more to do with Graeme dragging the family name down than his scotching their engagement.

"Well, not everyone," Julia grudgingly conceded and a twinkle returned to her emerald eyes. "Eleanor could not come, you see, because she's in the midst of wedding preparations!"

"For your brother?" Violet asked.

Julia smiled and shook her head. "No, her own!" She threw Brynnde a meaningful look. "Mama and Papa agreed to Thomas Dryer's suit!"

Brynnde gasped, and Julia nodded. "I know! But after everything, I suppose they no longer had the mettle for an argument. Mr. Dryer has money and a comfortable house. No land to speak of, but Eleanor plans to help him with his business, of all things, at least until there are children." Julia's pursed lips showed just what she thought of that.

Violet sat back in her chair. "My goodness."

"And where will Graeme and Lady Elisabeth settle?" Brynnde asked.

"Her family has handed over one of their properties for Graeme to manage. Papa has also given them a bit of land to build a second house on as the one on the Talmidge property is very old and hardly worth renovating." Julia glanced up surreptitiously at the crumbling medallion over the bed where she sat.

"So," Julia went on, "that only leaves me and Garrick."

"Will you have another Season?" Violet asked.

Julia shrugged. "Probably. Once Graeme and Elisabeth are properly established, everything will blow over. None of it will stick to me anyway."

"Or..." Brynnde forced her tongue away from his Christian name, "Lord Burbridge."

Julia cocked an eye at her. "And what about you? Does everyone think you've had a narrow escape with calumny?"

"Maman wants me to marry Mr. Dallweather," said Brynnde with a quick look at Violet.

Julia noticed and gave Violet a quick, speculative look as well before returning her attention to Brynnde. "But you would rather not." It was a statement, not a question.

"He is very kind, but we have nothing in common," Brynnde said. "He likes dogs but does not keep horses—"

"He would let you keep horses, though," Julia posited.

"I don't know," Brynnde admitted. "I suppose. He's much older—"

"Steady, then," said Julia. "Unlikely to wander."

Brynnde stared at her.

"I'm only imagining all the arguments being made for the match," Julia allowed. "All the reasons you don't want to marry him have claims in their favor as well."

"You should go into law," said Brynnde.

Julia laughed but then became serious. "Do you think they'll make you marry him?"

Brynnde shifted uncomfortably in her chair and looked again at where Violet stared intently out the window. "Papa won't rush me, but..."

"How soon?" Julia asked, leaning forward.

Brynnde turned a startled face to her. "What?"

"How soon would they demand you agree?"

Brynnde wriggled some more. "By Christmas, I would think. They'd like to announce it at the holiday ball, I'm sure."

Violet stood abruptly. "I'm just going to help Mama with tea," she said before fleeing.

Julia watched after her. "What's that about, I wonder? No prospects?"

Brynnde hesitated to give away a friend's secret but decided they must all be friends if they were going to stay at Lowlea together for any length of time. "She met Mr. Dallweather during a visit to Aux Arbres."

Julia's eyebrows nearly met her hairline. "Oh?"

"They got on quite nicely."

"Oh!"

"And if I hadn't needed to get away for a while, I'm sure both sides would have enjoyed furthering the acquaintance," said Brynnde.

"Well, that's one problem solved then," said Julia.

"What do you mean?" Brynnde asked.

"Let her have Mr. Dallweather," said Julia.

Brynnde found Julia's tone surprisingly irksome. Though she had already given Violet her blessing to win Mr. Dallweather, had in fact promised Violet a chance at him, the notion that Julia thought nothing of Brynnde being left alone and a spinster felt like a nail to her heart.

"Your parents could hardly press you to marry him if he were to turn his suit to Miss Crabbage," Julia went on. "You simply must do it before the holidays. Invite her back to Aux Arbres and maximize the time spent in Mr. Dallweather's company. Contrive—"

"Yes, we had thought of that, thank you," Brynnde put in crisply.

"We?" Julia asked.

"Violet and I have already discussed it. A little."

Julia smiled, warm and genuine. "I should have guessed you would have. Garrick says you're no slouch, which from him is very high praise." She jumped off the bed. "I suppose I'll go freshen myself up for tea." But before leaving, she embraced Brynnde once more. "It *is* good to see you!" And then she was gone in a blur, leaving Brynnde in a turmoil of emotions, like tangled yarn that she could not even begin to pick apart into discreet threads.

THE ENSUING DAYS showed Julia coming up with ever more elaborate plans for bringing Violet and Mr. Dallweather together. "She could fall from her horse—"

"I don't ride," Violet reminded her mildly. It was an unseasonably warm day, and they sat around the edge of the gurgling fountain. Violet had brought out a book and a few of the now drooping flowers, and she was pressing the best candidates between pages.

"Get lost in the woods then!" Julia exclaimed, clapping with joy over her own cleverness. "And he and his dogs can find you! Even better if it's raining." She looked up at the sky, but the day was bright and clear, offering only a cool breeze as a hint of autumn.

"She'll make herself sick, out in the cold and wet like that," said Brynnde as she yanked at some grass. "And Mr. Dallweather has a horror of sickness. His first wife died rather abruptly from pleurisy."

This gave Julia pause. "Does anyone die *abruptly* from pleurisy?" she wondered.

"I was very young," Brynnde admitted, "but it seemed Mrs. Dallweather had a cold one day and was dead the next."

Silence fell over them as they duly considered this. "Maybe not a rainy day then," Julia finally amended.

"I would rather not get lost," Violet ventured. "What if they did not find me?"

"Oh, they would," Julia assured her. "Love never gives

up, you know."

Bitterness flooded Brynnde's mouth at the words. Julia had not said any more about Garrick since the day she'd arrived, and why should she? There had been no real love between them. And so there was nothing to give up.

Except a life of her own rather than one at the mercy and sufferance of her family. Not for the first time she marveled at her desire to escape Aux Arbres, the very place she had fought to keep from leaving. Surely Nicolas would not throw her out, and if he were to marry Julia, so much the better; Julia would not rush her to the door either. But after being engaged and living for weeks under the idea of having her own household to run, Brynnde found it impossible now to consider subsisting forever at someone else's hand.

"I do not think Brynnde is ready to go home." Violet's gentle voice broke into Brynnde's thoughts.

Brynnde reached over and squeezed her friend's hand. "I am sorry," she said. "But I do promise not to be a burden here for too much longer, and then you can come and visit and establish a firmer acquaintance with Mr. Dallweather."

Violet gasped and removed her hand. "You are not a burden! It is so lovely to have company. Both of you," she craned to acknowledge Julia where she sat on the other side of Brynnde, "are welcome as long as—"

Oliver came tearing around the corner of the house and streaked across the patchy lawn. The three young ladies watched him pass. "Lowlea hasn't much of a future in him, I'm afraid," Violet sighed.

"Where is he going, I wonder?" asked Julia, stretching her neck to look over the fountain. "Is there anything that way but the gates?"

"He'll probably jump onto a passing cart and ride into town," said Violet as she carefully pressed another flower. "That is his usual gambit, especially when he has pocket money. He spends it all on sweets and comes home with a stomach ache."

"And what will you do with those?" Brynnde asked. "After they're pressed?"

Violet brightened slightly. "Sometimes I make cards, or I paint them onto my watercolors."

Julia settled once more on the grass. "Really? How remarkable."

"Oh, yes, there's so much you can do with them," Violet said, warming to her subject. "Decoupage, or even just arranging them behind glass."

Brynnde pictured Belle Weather filled with dried flower art. It did not seem out of place in her mind. "You're quite artful," she told Violet.

Her friend blushed. "There aren't so many things to do here," she said. "I read a lot, and walk, and..." She gestured at the book and flowers.

"And paint, and decoupage, and probably also do needlework," Julia added. "Brynnde is right, you really are inventive, coming up with so many ways to fill your time."

"I fear it's boring here for you, however," said Violet.

"It's only nice to be away from Ridgemow for a bit," said Julia, "with two weddings to plan. And I'm tired of only having Ellie to talk to, and hardly her at all these days either."

Brynnde detected an inkling of sadness behind Julia's seemingly light tone. "You'll miss her, I suppose."

Julia tossed her head. "She won't be far." It rang of words said regularly, Brynnde thought, as though Julia were trying to convince herself that not much would change. How strange it must be to be so close to one's sister. Brynnde rather hoped that when Tessa married she would move far, far away and only return to Aux Arbres at Christmas.

"Perhaps not," said Brynnde, addressing Julia, "but I'm sure she expects to be busy establishing her household and helping with her husband's business as well. And with your brothers gone, too..."

Julia's brow furrowed. "Graeme will be gone, but Garrick isn't planning to go anywhere. With Graeme no longer around to run Ridgemow, Garrick will have no choice but to stay home."

Brynnde wondered whether Garrick shared his sister's certainty on the subject. In Brynnde's experience, Garrick did what he liked, and it was established he liked to travel and had less interest in tending the family estate.

Violet snapped her book shut and squinted at the unforgiving sky. "It is unnaturally warm today."

Brynnde and Julia agreed, but as they stood and shook the grass from their skirts, Julia unexpectedly kicked off her boots, and before Brynnde or Violet could ask why, Julia hopped into the fountain.

"That feels much better!" said Julia, her dress held up in fistfuls of fabric.

"Your stockings!" Violet cried. "They'll be ruined!"

Julia shrugged. "Stockings are easily replaced," she said, and Brynnde grimaced, thinking it might be true for the Sommerfords and Archambaults but not necessarily true for the Crabbages.

"Come on!" said Julia.

Brynnde exchanged a glance with Violet and was surprised when Violet squared her shoulders and dropped her book. Brynnde relaxed a bit when she saw that Violet moved to take off her stockings as well as her boots; not all good sense had left her friend. Brynnde followed suit, and soon all three of them were wading in the cool spill of the fountain. They were careful at first, and slow, but before long were kicking up small sprays of water and enjoying the sparkling arcs in the sunlight. Then Julia began to dance a jig.

It was refreshing, Brynnde thought—not only the water, but to be doing something so different. If Lady Crabbage were to see them, they would assuredly receive a lecture. And if Sir Everett were to catch them, Brynnde could hardly imagine what might occur. Would he be more outraged at their behavior or at any perceived damage to his expensive statuary?

Violet's thoughts appeared to go in a similar direction, and she stepped to the lip of the fountain and back down onto the grass. Brynnde turned to do the same, but Julia grabbed her arm and laughingly swung her into her dance. Though normally an adept dance partner, in this instance Brynnde was taken off guard—and off balance. She spun and landed on her bottom in the water, her skirts buoyed briefly like Ophelia's, then sinking.

Beside her, Julia gabbled. "I'm so sorry! Oh, Brynnde, please forgive me! I'm so sorry! Are you all right?"

"I'm fine," Brynnde assured, "only wet." She shivered. Though the cool had felt good on her bare feet, it felt far chillier now that it soaked her skirts and shift. The day no longer seemed so warm.

Later Brynnde could scarce remember how she managed to get out of the fountain and back to the house, and if Lady Crabbage did lecture them it fell on deaf ears. By then Brynnde's shivers had become head-rattling shakes, and she was sent to bed with tea and broth and the expense of a roaring fire.

Well, Brynnde thought as she succumbed to the kind of exhaustion particular to acute illness, *at least I needn't feel bad about feigning illness.* She would have called Molly to bring her paper and a pen to write Nicolas but was asleep before her hand touched the bell.

18

———

There was much murmuring around her, and occasionally hands on her that she feebly attempted to push away. Why were all these people in her room? She only wanted to rest. At one point she felt sure Garrick was there, leaning over her, brushing back the sweat-damp hair from her forehead. Would he kiss her? But no, he didn't. How infuriating.

When she opened her eyes, morning light greeted her from the window, and Brynnde supposed she'd been dreaming. No wonder she did not feel at all rested. She struggled weakly to a sitting position and reached for the bell but only managed to knock it off the bedside table. It landed on the rug with a muffled clank. She bent to reach for it but immediately felt dizzy and was on the verge of falling out of bed entirely when the door banged open.

Strong hands righted her, pushing Brynnde back against her pillow, but it took a few moments more before her head stopped spinning and she could make sense of the stormy eyes glaring down at her. "Garrick!" she said, not thinking to use his proper title. "I mean, Lord Bur—"

He scowled. "Never mind that. What did you think you were doing, playing about in cold water in autumn?"

"It was hot and—what are you doing here?" Brynnde asked.

"I came the same day Julia's letter arrived."

"Julia's letter?" Brynnde shook her head, not comprehending his meaning. "How could she have written to you already?"

Garrick's rigid stance relaxed slightly. "You have been ill for over a week," he informed her. "Julia was none too well herself for a couple days, but you seem to have borne the worst of it."

Conveniently forgetting her plan to feign illness, Brynnde wondered what right Garrick had to scold her, as though she'd purposefully meant to fall ill? But she pursed her lips against the outburst forming and instead said, "That does not answer my question."

Garrick's brow furrowed in a show of confusion.

"Why are you here?" Brynnde asked.

"I told you, Julia wrote me. But if you're asking about just now, I heard the bell fall." He nodded to the bell, now restored to its rightful place; Brynnde guessed he had picked it up when he'd righted her earlier.

"How could you have?" she wondered. "Even Molly didn't hear."

"She is down in the kitchens. I—" Garrick cleared his throat and changed the subject. "Should I send for her? You must be parched at the very least. I am sorry for not attending to you sooner." He seemed suddenly eager to get away, walking crablike in the direction of the door, which he had left ajar. "Your brother is also here," he added, hand on the knob.

Nicolas! Oh, and Julia here as well! Brynnde clapped her hands together, a smile lighting her wan face.

Garrick's brows lowered once more. "You are eager to see him," he surmised. "Would you like me to fetch him?"

"Oh, yes!" said Brynnde, only afterward thinking to add, "Please."

Garrick executed a stiff bow punctuated with a curious frown and left the room, softly closing the door behind him and leaving Brynnde to her thoughts.

She hadn't been dreaming after all. The hands on her must have been the physician, possibly Molly or other maids... And that dream of Garrick touching her forehead? Brynnde suddenly felt overly warm under the blankets. She squirmed and reached again for the bell, thinking to ask Molly to bring up water for her to wash in, but then her eyes fell on the folded paper sticking out of the book that also rested on the table—Garrick's note.

A fresh well of irritation sprang up in Brynnde's chest. She need not look at the note to remember the words. *Former friendliness.* Is that what had brought him to Lowlea? More likely he'd been worried for his sister's sake rather than Brynnde's. Yes, he would come to attend Julia just as Nicolas—

As if responding to Brynnde's thoughts, the door opened again, this time revealing her brother. His dark hair was more disheveled even than usual, there were dark circles under his eyes, and his coquelicot waistcoat looked ridiculous paired with damson breeches. "You must have come without Martin to dress you," Brynnde remarked.

"What?" asked Nicolas. He glanced down at himself. "Oh." Then he shook his head and sighed. "Honestly, Bryn, I thought you were only going to pretend to take ill."

"You know me," said Brynnde, "I never do things by halves."

"You might have considered it, just this once." He stepped further into the room and closed the door. "Do you think you can eat?"

"I'd like to wash up first," Brynnde said. "I was just about to ring for Molly."

"No need," said Nicolas. "I believe Burbridge already went down to set her about her business. And Lady Crabbage is calling for the physician again. I'll write home to let them know your progress." Brynnde read in the slope of her brother's shoulders his relief at being able to tell their parents she was awake and recovering.

"Was I really ill for a week?" she asked.

"This is the eighth day," Nicolas told her. "I wasn't going to be able to prevent Papa from coming here himself much longer."

"Papa!" Her condition must have been worse than she originally thought if her father would have come.

"Yes, well," Nicolas turned toward the door. "If I get a letter off to him this morning..."

"Wait!"

Nicolas looked back at his sister.

"What about Julia?"

A hunted expression settled over Nicolas' features. "She is well. She was only ill a couple of days."

"And?" Brynnde prompted.

Nicolas remained resolutely silent.

"I will have a relapse here and now if you do not tell me how you are getting on with her!"

"We have had a number of pleasant conversations, and she is a good partner at cards," Nicolas reported. "But naturally most of my energy has been tied up in concerns for you, dear sister, so if you will allow me..."

"Change your clothes before you see her!" Brynnde called after him, but the door had already closed. She slumped against her pillows, her gaze falling once again on the note from Garrick. According to Nicolas, Garrick had gone to fetch Molly for her. How... *friendly*.

There came a tap at the door. "Yes?" Brynnde called, and the door swung open yet again, this time with Molly behind it. The maid carried a tray of dry toast and water. "Can't start you off too strong too soon," Molly said as she set the tray beside the bed, brushing the book and bell aside to make space. "Your stomach would kick up a riot for sure."

"I'd really rather wash up, Molly," said Brynnde.

"Oh, I've got that coming up next," Molly assured her. "But you need your strength to get up and moving."

Brynnde obliged by nibbling some toast. "Did..." She reminded herself to use his title, "Lord Burbridge send you?"

Molly eyed her thoughtfully, and Brynnde had to fight not to fidget amidst the linens. "He did," the maid answered at length, adding, "It's a wonder he heard you, but then he is only across the hall."

"I dropped the bell," said Brynnde.

"So Lord Burbridge said. Still and all, he shouldn't have been in here alone with you."

The insinuation caused Brynnde's heart to pick up speed, though she couldn't have said whether it angered or excited her. "The door was open!"

Molly grimaced. "Not as like I'm going to tell tales," she said.

"Molly!"

The maid smiled. "Now don't work yourself up. It's clear to anyone you've not done nothing."

Brynnde was disconcerted by the dart of disappointment Molly's words delivered. "What do you mean?"

"Miss, you've been sick for a week now. You have no strength for..." She blushed and looked away. "Shenanigans."

Brynnde's mouth fell open, but no words were forthcoming. She could hardly upbraid Molly for coming to a correct conclusion, and she had never scolded Molly for being familiar nor had any inclination to start now. Molly was, after all, the sister Tessa was not—the person Brynnde could tell things to and know her secrets would be kept.

"And you're a good girl," Molly declared, "so I know you would never. But him, what might he do? Who can say?"

Brynnde melted under Molly's fierce concern. "Oh, Molly, it's really all right. Lord Burbridge only wishes to be a friend. He's told me so himself." *In that wretched letter.*

Molly's brow furrowed, her eyes narrowing with suspicion. "But he was to marry you!"

"Only to keep me from having to become Mrs. Dallweather." When Molly's expression remained unconvinced, Brynnde insisted, "He would never force himself on a lady."

"What one brother may do..." said Molly.

"So might another?" Brynnde finished then shook her head. "Not in this case, Molly. You've seen how different they are."

Molly sniffed audibly. "You eat that, and I'll be back up with some water for washing." And she turned on her heel and left, clicking the door firmly closed behind her.

THAT AFTERNOON, Dr. Shepherd decreed it would be all

right for Brynnde to establish herself in the parlour so long as she did not exert herself overmuch. And so she found herself so surrounded by pillows as to almost be pushed off the settee by them and wrapped in a shawl that made her appear to be wearing a bed sheet. Indeed, Garrick smiled when he saw her and said, "And here we have the Empress of Rome in full toga. No, no! Do not remove it! I'm sure Lady Crabbage will faint if you do not follow the doctor's orders to the letter. If he says you must wear a toga, then…" He spread his hands, palms up, in a show of helplessness.

On the opposite sofa, Julia rolled her eyes. "My brother thinks he's very funny."

Garrick arched a brow at her. "I do hope you had the grace to apologize to Miss Archambault for your bad influence given that was the cause of her collapse."

Julia's cheeks flamed. "I was ill too!" But then she slumped back under her brother's fulsome glare. "And yes, of course I have. And Brynnde has forgiven me. Haven't you?"

"Most assuredly," Brynnde agreed. "It's not as if Julia forced me to do it," she told Garrick. "If she made a miscalculation, so did I."

"And here I thought you were good at maths," said Garrick as he nudged his sister over a bit so he could sit. "Julia, on the other hand…"

"I'm better at numbers than Ellie," Julia said. "I don't know how she can hope to help run a business."

"Leave it be," said Garrick mildly, still smiling, but Brynnde detected tension beneath the words. She found herself searching his expression and caught his eye, but like a cat he lazily turned his head and looked away. With his gaze fixed on the tall windows, he asked, "So what shall you do, Miss Archambault? Spend your days reading until you are released to return home? Do needlepoint?"

"Violet has no shortage of books," answered Brynnde. "And my fingers would prefer to stay clear of needles just now. When will you return to Ridgemow?"

"Julia wanted to be sure of your recovery," said Garrick, and Julia swiveled in his direction, mouth agape. "As did I," he amended before his sister could unleash her complaint.

Brynnde's mind flew. If she wanted to be sure of Nicolas' attachment to Julia, she would have to get her and Garrick to stay for at least a couple more days. "I do wonder where my brother has disappeared to," she remarked. "Of anyone, he should be the most concerned for my health."

"Oh, he has been!" Julia assured.

Garrick pulled back slightly at Julia's vehemence. With an odd look at his sister, he said, "Indeed, he has been unwilling to leave the house for want of being the first to hear any news of your condition."

An idea struck Brynnde then. Garrick had helped with Eleanor's beau, why could he not help with Julia's? Her eyes lit up at the thought, and both Garrick and Julia blinked at her from the opposite couch, matching expressions of wariness on their faces.

"Are you feeling entirely well, Miss Archambault?" Garrick asked. "Have you overexerted yourself?"

Brynnde only just stopped herself bouncing where she sat, so eager was she to tell Garrick of her plan. How could she get him alone so they could discuss it?

"You do look a bit feverish," said Julia. "Perhaps my brother would be so kind as to help you back upstairs for some rest."

This time, Garrick's mouth dropped open as though to protest, but upon meeting Julia's pointed gaze, he snapped it shut again. "I'm sure he is a perfect gentleman and will not compromise you," Julia said sternly.

Brynnde remembered Molly's words that morning and felt her cheeks grow hot. "Of course he wouldn't! He is not —" She bit down on Graeme's name and finished weakly, "like that."

Garrick grimaced. "Were that all gentlemen were so well behaved," he muttered then rose. "Come then, Miss Archambault. Let me help you up the stairs." He took Brynnde's hand and helped her to stand, a torrent of pillows rolling free like a soft avalanche as she dislodged herself. Then Garrick straightened the oversized shawl around Brynnde's shoulders and, with a swift, shrewd glare at his sister, led her from the parlour.

19

*B*rynnde could hardly wait to tell Garrick her scheme. "We must talk," she said as they reached the staircase.

Garrick lifted an eyebrow. "Please contain yourself, Miss Archambault, or I fear you may relapse. And I would hate to be to blame for it."

"What? No, I'm fine." But her slight wobble as they made their way up the stairs belied her words. She felt Garrick's hand tighten on hers.

"Careful," he said.

"It's—" Brynnde stopped to glance around and make sure no one was in hearing. "It's Nicolas and Julia, you see."

Garrick made a show of glancing around as well. "No, I don't see."

"Of course you don't; you haven't been paying attention." She teetered again and Garrick placed a hand on the small of her back to keep her from tipping backward.

"Julia has formed a *tendre* for Nicolas," said Brynnde.

Garrick's brows came down. "She told you this?"

"Yes," said Brynnde, "and I believe Nicolas is likewise not indifferent toward her, either. So you see—"

"What a little matchmaker you are," Garrick said, urging her gently up the stairs. "First Eleanor and now Julia. And I suppose you have someone in mind for Miss Crabbage as well?"

"Actually—"

"Oh, dear Lord, I was joking!"

Brynnde drew back and risked toppling. "I only thought you might like to see your sister happy. Perhaps I was mistaken." She moved to step away from Garrick's grasp, but he held firm.

"Of course I want to see her happy," Garrick said as he propelled Brynnde up the final few stairs. "But after everything between our families..." He shook his head then stopped short and looked hard at Brynnde. "And what of you?"

"What of me?" Brynnde asked.

"You're so set on everyone else's happiness. What about yours?"

"Oh, but it makes me happy to see them happy," said Brynnde. "If Violet marries Mr. Dallweather, I won't have to. And if Julia marries Nicolas, I'm sure they'll let me stay at Aux Arbres."

Garrick's slate eyes seemed to boil with dark clouds. "Is that what you want? To stay at Aux Arbres for the rest of your life? A spinster?"

"I don't see that I have very many options," Brynnde told him. "I only know what I don't want, which is to be Mrs. Dallweather."

"Anything but that," Garrick said grimly. "Any*one* but that, eh?"

Brynnde did not understand his sudden ire, the way his

lips went thin and eyes flashed. She recoiled, this time successfully snatching back her arm from his. "I did believe you wanted to be friends, Lord Burbridge," she said, and for once the formality of his title felt just right. "But perhaps you wrote that note thinking we might never have to meet again in person. Thank you for helping me up the stairs. I can make it to my room on my own."

She turned and half stumbled down the hallway, her vision blurred by the threat of tears.

NOT WILLING TO GO BACK TO bed so soon, Brynnde instead ensconced herself on the window seat that overlooked the wilds of the back garden. She watched Oliver scamper about while Master Collins hung back, clearly reproaching his charge but reluctant to venture into the tall grass. Before long, Oliver was out of sight and Master Collins had given up and gone back inside the house. Brynnde wondered whether the boy ever actually learned anything.

A few minutes later, a familiar glint of golden hair caught Brynnde's flagging attention. Garrick stepped outside, Violet on his arm. Behind him came Nicolas and Julia. The foursome picked their way along the broken, rutted path, the gentlemen holding the ladies' arms so that they would not trip on the cracks and swells. Brynnde watched as Nicolas smiled down at Julia beside him—a genuine smile, not his polite, enduring one—and she chattered animatedly up at him. But though Brynnde knew she should be pleased, she could not stop looking at the way Garrick smiled so indulgently at Violet as well.

Garrick was a rescuer; Brynnde knew as much from experience. Perhaps after seeing Lowlea he had concluded Violet needed saving? She would be easy to live with—

uncomplaining, sweet Violet. Smart enough to run a house, and she'd never beg to go traveling with Garrick, so he would be free to go where and do whatever he liked. And when she blushed like that, Violet was remarkably pretty.

Something swelled in Brynnde's throat that felt unexpectedly like heartache. She told herself it had nothing to do with Garrick's apparent interest in Violet but instead was prompted by the understanding that, should Violet become attached to Garrick, Brynnde would be stuck with Mr. Dallweather. Again.

Brynnde stared out the window, unseeing, long past the point the others had become obscured from view. Her mind whirled. If she were to decline Mr. Dallweather and stay at Aux Arbres—ever assuming that Nicolas and Julia (for Brynnde was determined those two were firmly fixed) would allow her to stay—how awkward life would become. Brynnde would upset the friendly balance of the neighborhood, never mind being the third wheel at Aux Arbres. Oh, Nicolas and Julia would never treat her as such, but Brynnde knew she'd feel it anyway. Every visit to the tenants would be laced with the unspoken censure: "She should have taken Mr. Dallweather, he's a good man," and, "She's a spinster now, poor thing, when she had a good offer too." The neighbors would sympathize with Mr. Dallweather as the hurt party... Brynnde felt the walls closing in on her. She'd be unable to visit people without feeling their judgement, unable to live at home without feeling like a burden... She was as like as not to become a shut-in.

Meanwhile, Violet would be mistress of Ridgemow. Brynnde had not seen the estate, but she imagined it anyway, made frothy and gleaming from inner fantasy. Feeling sorry for Brynnde, Violet would invite her to visit, and Brynnde would be forced to witness the happy union of

Lord and Lady Burbridge. The very notion made the knot in Brynnde's throat harder, until she felt as though she'd attempted to swallow an egg whole.

Such were the lines of her thoughts when Molly bustled in. "Oh, Miss," the maid said upon seeing her, "should I call for the doctor? You look that peaky. Feeling sick again? Here, you should come rest in bed..."

Brynnde waved off Molly's reaching hands. "No, Molly, no more bed. I'm only watching everyone walk through the garden."

Molly leaned toward the glass for a look. "I don't see as anyone's there," she said, then eyed Brynnde with fresh concern. "Could it be you're seeing things now?"

"They're not there now, but they were, and they will return at some point," said Brynnde.

"Well'm, would you like a book or some tea while you wait?" Molly asked.

"No thank you, Molly." But as the maid turned to go, Brynnde could not stop herself from asking, "Molly, have you heard any... Talk? About Lord Burbridge and Miss Crabbage?"

Molly turned around and cocked her head. "Miss?"

"Are the servants saying anything?" Brynnde asked, twisting the shawl that shrouded her with her fingers. She hated even asking the question, but she had to know. The sooner she had facts, the sooner she could sort out her own feelings and decide her next course of action.

"About Lord Burbridge and Miss Crabbage?" Molly asked. "I only know they went out for a walk with Master Nicolas and Lady Julia. Oh! Is that who you were looking for there? You must feel awful lonely being unable to go out and all." Molly came back and dared to sit on the edge of the window seat. For the first time in her life, Brynnde really looked at her maid. Red hair sticking out from under her cap, green-gray eyes, and a smattering of freckles. Brynnde often forgot Molly wasn't much older than her. Molly just *was*, a steady and reliable presence.

All at once, Brynnde could not hold back the tears. She put her face in her hands and cried. "Oh, Molly, what am I to do?"

Molly jumped to her feet and patted Brynnde awkwardly. "Oh, Miss, it's all right. You'll be well enough soon and can walk with your friends then."

Brynnde shook her head, unable to articulate her deep fears.

"He's right," Brynnde finally managed. "Our families can no longer have any attachment between them. He will marry Violet, and oh! Poor Nicolas and Julia!"

This time Molly plunked herself down firmly beside Brynnde. "You're worried Lord Burbridge has an idea to go for Miss Crabbage? Well, that's just silly. The man's been wearing a hole in the carpet outside your door this past week, he won't be going after someone else now you're well."

Brynnde lifted her head, eyes wide with astonishment. "What? No, you must be exaggerating to make me feel better. Please, Molly, it would be much kinder to tell me the truth."

"Have I ever lied to you, Miss?" Molly reproved. "Your own brother wasn't half as worried about you as was Lord Burbridge. Then again, I warrant Master Nicolas was a wee distracted. Torn, as it was."

Movement outside the window drew Brynnde's attention, and Molly followed her gaze. The party were returning from their walk. Violet was becomingly flushed from the autumn air, and Garrick continued to smile at her as she talked. Nicolas, meanwhile, was laughing at something Julia was saying.

"They make a handsome couple," Molly mused.

A fresh stab of sorrow cut through Brynnde. "Yes."

Molly nudged her with an elbow. "I mean your brother and Lady Julia. Anyhow, I thought you weren't so fixed on Lord Burbridge except as a way to avoid becoming Mrs. Dallweather."

Brynnde grimaced then gasped as she understood Garrick's words on the stairs that morning. *Anyone but that.* Had Garrick been upset that Brynnde had agreed to marry him solely to get out of marrying someone else? Ridiculous! He'd been the one to propose, after all. Still... "Molly," Brynnde said, "how do you know when you're in love?"

Molly blushed and clasped her hands together. "Oh, Miss, there are a lot of kinds of love. Sometimes it happens all at once like lightning. And sometimes it takes a while. But you know it when you realize that person is someone you think about a lot and miss when they're gone. They're the person you want to tell things to, and show things, and do things with. Or so I'm told."

Brynnde could hear the chatter downstairs as the foursome came inside. "Molly," she said shrewdly as she took in her maid's downcast gaze, "have you been in love? Are you in love now?"

Molly's cheeks grew redder. "Well'm... Mayhap so, but..."

"Who? Someone I know?"

"Lord Burbridge has a valet by the name of Geoffrey. He's older than me for certain, but oh! Such the nicest man! And he tells the most amazing stories of all their travels. We met at the house party last spring, and now here again too, and so we haven't spent so much time together in the same place, but..."

"It was the lightning kind of love," Brynnde said. Molly nodded. "And does he feel, um, struck by lightning too?"

Molly nodded again and Brynnde sighed. No wonder Molly wanted her to believe Garrick had stronger feelings for her than simple friendship; if Garrick and Brynnde were to make a match, Molly could be with Geoffrey.

Still, Brynnde couldn't fault her maid for seeing things through love-blurred vision. Molly meant no harm by it. She would never purposely seek to hurt Brynnde's feelings by giving her false hope.

A tap at the door rushed Molly to her feet, their coze at an end. Molly opened the door and Julia stepped inside, positively aglow and oblivious to the misery hiding behind Brynnde's thin smile.

"Oh!" Julia said, throwing herself down beside Brynnde, "we've just been out for a walk. The weather is still remarkably fine for this time of year. But," she added as she turned toward the window, "you must have seen us! Did you? If I'd known, I would have waved." She looked at Brynnde. "Are you all right? Still fatigued? Why aren't you saying anything?"

Brynnde could not help laughing; at least if Julia were to become her sister-in-law she would never want for cheer. "Because you haven't given me a chance!" She grew sober again. If Garrick was right, there could be no match between Nicolas and Julia. The rift was unbridgeable. She should never have planned such a scheme as getting them together at Lowlea, for now the pain of parting would be all the greater.

"What's wrong?" Julia asked.

Brynnde struggled to smile. "I only wish I could have

joined you on your walk." It was not entirely untrue. Brynnde's natural disposition railed against being still and remaining indoors. She pictured Mr. Dallweather's overstuffed, too warm sitting room and suppressed a shudder; no, she could not live cooped up like that.

Julia, however, brightened. "I am sorry you had to miss it. It was lovely..." Her green eyes clouded with the memory, but then she snapped to. "I do think your brother may appreciate my sense of humor," she said. "You can't imagine how refreshing that is! *Now* what's wrong? Is it that I'm talking about it and you're still sorry you couldn't go?"

Brynnde bit her lip, unsure whether to voice her fears. But Julia's frank and steady gaze gave her courage. After all, Julia was not one to tiptoe or bandy. With a deep breath, Brynnde said, "Your brother said there could be no match between our families now. Not after... You know..."

Julia's brows came down and bright spots appeared on her cheeks, not the heat of embarrassment but anger. Brynnde recoiled, but soon discovered the anger was not directed at her. "Does he? I'm sure our family isn't in a position to be choosey at the moment, and if Nicolas were to ask for me, they could not say no. Nor would I."

Brynnde could not be surprised by Julia's use of Nicolas' Christian name; hadn't she used Garrick's in her own mind? She reached over and squeezed Julia's hands, but Julia quickly extracted them, new concern writ sharp across her dainty features. "Unless you think Nicolas would not dare offer because of what happened with you and Garrick?"

"I don't know," Brynnde replied honestly. "Nicolas has said he's in no hurry to marry. Maybe, with time, everything will blow over and it will no longer matter what happened this past Season."

Julia twisted her hands in her lap, and Brynnde

regretted shattering her sunny mood. "My parents may let me skip next Season to give people time enough to forget, but then they will insist on my going the following year." She looked hopefully at Brynnde. "Would he be ready by then?"

"Even if he isn't, I don't think Papa would give him any longer than that," said Brynnde. "He's twenty-four already, and Papa is keen to see us all settled." A small, dark cloud drifted across Brynnde's heart. She understood her father's desire to arrange things, but the knowledge of why—that he was aging and would not be around forever—saddened her. Worse would be to disappoint him.

"Well, at least you're one less thing for your father to worry about," said Julia.

Brynnde blinked at her in surprise. "What do you mean? That I should marry Mr. Dallweather?" Brynnde sighed. "I might would, just to ease Papa's mind, but I could not do that to Violet. She is so taken with him! And they are truly made for one another, I believe."

Julia stared at Brynnde as if she'd taken leave of her senses. "Mr. Dallweather? Of course you can't marry him! You must marry Garrick."

It was Brynnde's turn to look at Julia as if she'd gone mad. "Our engagement has been broken," she said, uncertain of how Julia could not know this.

"If I can marry your brother, you can marry mine," said Julia.

Brynnde wished she felt as confident as Julia on the matter, but it seemed that a betrothal, once broken, could not easily be repaired. Nicolas and Julia faced no such obstacle, but if Brynnde and Garrick were to marry—after all that had happened—it would only bring old ghosts and gossip back from where it should be safely buried. As it stood, the two of them at Lowlea together would surely make a tasty tidbit for Lady Crabbage to chew on. Perhaps a match between Nicolas and Julia would cause some of the same, but not on nearly the scale.

"Unless," Julia ventured, "you do not wish to marry Garrick?"

Brynnde turned wide eyes on her friend. "It's not that!" she asserted. In truth, she did not know whether she wanted to marry Garrick Sommerford; it seemed an impossibility and so she had not given any thought to it. "I only think it more likely he does not wish to marry me."

"Of course he does!" cried Julia. "He would not have asked you otherwise, you goose!"

Brynnde supposed it was as good a time as any to tell the entire story. "He was only being kind, you see," she said as she finished. "Gallant, really. He has no particular desire to marry me and probably feels he's had a narrow escape."

Julia eyed Brynnde with suspicion. "I do not believe it is as simple as that," she said. "Even if what you say is true, Garrick would not have insisted on staying here if he had not been truly concerned for you. We'd have long since returned to Ridgemow. And do you know, this is the longest he's been home since gaining his majority that I can remember?"

"Well, he must stay home now, mustn't he?" Brynnde asked. "He will have to learn to run Ridgemow if Graeme is leaving."

But Julia shook her head. "Believe me, if Garrick wants to escape a place or person, he'll find the means."

Brynnde recalled what Molly had said about Garrick being so worried for her while she'd been sick. Could it be that his feelings for her extended beyond friendship? Yet his note to her suggested otherwise. "He was probably only feeling responsible for my poor condition," she said aloud, half to herself.

"Guilty by association? Because he is my brother?" Julia laughed and shook her head again. "Garrick never minds leaving us to our own disasters. And before you tell me he only came here to make sure *I* was well," she added as Brynnde opened her mouth to find yet another excuse for Garrick's behavior, "I can promise you he's never half worried about me, Ellie, or Graeme the way he worried for you this past week. Why, I haven't seen him so worked up since his prize hunter went lame!"

Brynnde failed to stifle her yelp of mirth at being likened to a horse. Julia grimaced. "Not that you deserve such a comparison," she said earnestly. "But Garrick cares more for his horses than just about anything. They are the only things he misses when he is away from Ridgemow."

"Oh, no, I find it quite flattering," Brynnde teased.

Julia smiled and stood. "Will you be well enough to join us for dinner this evening?"

Brynnde nodded. "I do not intend to be left out of any more of the fun," she declared.

Julia gave Brynnde's hand a final squeeze before leaving. "Good. Violet is sweet, but I have missed your company."

"Even with Nicolas here?" Brynnde asked in astonishment.

Julia's lips twisted. "Certainly, he has done his best to be entertaining."

"You make it sound as though he has failed."

"Quite the opposite," said Julia. "If he makes himself any more charming I will throw myself at his head and make a cake of myself. Which is why I need you, dear Brynnde." She turned shining green eyes to her friend, "Oh," she breathed, her usual playful façade slipping, "I made such fun of Ellie for feeling this way, and I only hope you will feel it too one day!"

Brynnde looked at Julia's pained expression and said, "You make it look as though it hurts to be in love."

"It does!" Julia said, "but in the most pleasant way!" And with that she all but skipped out of the room.

---

20

*B*rynnde took particular care with her toilette before dinner that evening. She told herself this was because she wanted to look well and not cause any further alarm about her health. The better she looked, and the more energetic she behaved, the sooner Dr. Shepherd would give her leave to go outside and eventually travel home to Aux Arbres.

The thought of going home tore Brynnde in two. Part of her felt the sooner she got away from Garrick, the better. Being around him mixed her up, and Brynnde yearned to go back to her more carefree days of riding and not thinking about, well, much of anyone really.

However, she also knew returning to Aux Arbres would mean facing the decision about Mr. Dallweather. If she brought Violet with her, there was a fair chance her friend would distract the gentleman and divert his fancy. Then Brynnde really would be able to go back to her old life.

Except something told Brynnde life would never be the same as it used to be, no matter what happened.

"Drat it," she hissed, slamming her silver brush onto the vanity table. Her hair would not behave the way she wished.

Without a word, Molly stepped over, took up the brush, and began to work on Brynnde's dark tresses. She twisted and pinned with rapid efficiency. "There now, Miss," she said a few minutes later.

Brynnde could hardly believe what she saw. "Why, Molly! That's amazing!" She turned one way then the other in her chair, eyeing herself in the glass. "I did not know you were so capable. Why have you never said?"

The maid blushed with pleasure at the praise. "Because you always do for yourself. But you see, Miss, how sometimes letting someone do for you is not so terrible, eh? Now let's get you into this dress."

It was mulberry colored and trimmed in much brilliant white lace, and it managed to make Brynnde's lingering pallor appear merely pale, especially once she applied a bit of rouge. If nothing else, Brynnde thought, having been ill had made her eyes look bigger and brighter than ever.

The dinner bell rang, and Brynnde went down to the drawing room to join the others. Lady Crabbage was in a dither, as usual, and Sir Everret appeared stunned to have so many people in his house. For his sake alone, Brynnde wished again to return to Aux Arbres, if only to relieve Sir Everret's burden.

She did not have long to consider her host, however, as Violet came to see her. "I am so sorry I did not come sooner," she said, brown eyes shining. "With so many people in the house, it is all I can do to keep Mama sane."

"I understand," said Brynnde. Lady Crabbage loved company, and it fell to Violet to both help host and prevent her mother from suffocating her guests with her expansive personality. "Were you the one to suggest a walk earlier? I could do with fresh air myself."

Violet glanced apprehensively at her mother. "Mama would be beside herself if you went out before Dr. Shepherd permitted."

Brynnde sighed. It would not do to upset her hosts; she'd done enough by being foolish and getting sick. "Don't worry," she assured Violet, "I promise to stay put until Dr. Shepherd says it is safe."

The steward came then to tell them dinner was ready. The introduction of Lord Burbridge and Nicolas had necessarily caused a change of seating, Brynnde discovered, with Lady Crabbage subscribing to the fashion of alternating the gentlemen and ladies. This placed Brynnde next to Garrick and across from Nicolas who, she was pleased to note, was beside Julia. Violet sat on Nicolas' other side, and to prevent the arrangements from being lopsided, Master Collins had been invited to join them as well. Brynnde had not noticed him in the drawing room; indeed, she thought he was the kind to be overlooked just about anywhere he went. The tutor was short and soberly dressed with something of a mournful aspect about him, and Brynnde wondered whether it was Master Collins' natural disposition or Oliver had worn him down to such. In either case, he did not speak much, eyes always downcast as though somehow reading his soup.

Still, Brynnde endeavored to hold some kind of conversation with Master Collins, the alternative being to favor Garrick on her other side. After their last encounter, she could not be sure he wanted her attention, nor was she quite ready to accept his. Brynnde was aware of her brother's and Julia's odd glances from across the table as she attempted again and again to draw Master Collins out. At the same time, she could hear the low rumble of Garrick's voice on her other side as he occasionally responded to Lady Crabbage. Never once did Garrick address her, which only made Brynnde more determined to win Master Collins over.

"Warwickshire is no little distance from here," she said upon extracting Master Collins' origins. "Do you visit your family often?"

"I haven't any," he said in his low, mournful way, leaving their conversation at yet another impasse.

Lady Crabbage swooped in with alacrity. "Master Collins comes to us through my aunt's nephew, by which I mean the unrelated side of our family."

Brynnde blinked, unable to determine if this meant some branch of Lady Crabbage's family were somehow all dead. Should she offer condolences? Nor could she entirely decipher whether Master Collins was himself the nephew or only related to the nephew. "Wouldn't your aunt's nephew be your cousin?" she asked.

"Oh, no, not in the least!" said Lady Crabbage without elaborating, leaving Brynnde more mystified than ever.

Finally the meal ended and Brynnde escaped only to be thrown into a fresh fire once the ladies had withdrawn to the parlour. Without preamble, Julia took Brynnde aside and asked, "Why would you not speak to Garrick at dinner?"

"He was occupied with Lady Crabbage," Brynnde protested, though she knew her argument was weak. "And I felt that poor Master Collins could do with some encouragement."

Julia's eyes narrowed, and Brynnde knew she was trying to decide whether to believe her. "Well," she said at last, "you will at least have the opportunity to converse once the gentlemen join us."

Brynnde smiled in a way she hoped showed pleasure at

the prospect, even as her stomach cramped around the mutton she'd just eaten. She was much relieved when Violet joined them. "Your appetite appears to be returning," she said to Brynnde.

Brynnde detected the hopeful note in her friend's voice. "Yes," she said, "and I'm sure Dr. Shepherd will be releasing me in no time. And then *you* will come back to Aux Arbres." She did not need to elaborate.

Violet smiled and flushed. "Oh, thank you!"

"Thank *you*, dear Violet," said Brynnde. "I'm only sorry to have made you wait so long."

Julia smiled as well. "Oh, I do hope it all goes to plan! I met Mr. Dallweather only briefly during our stay at Aux Arbres, but it does seem the two of you are well suited." She seemed about to say more, but the gentlemen entered then, and all Julia's attention bent toward Nicolas. Brynnde smiled to see it.

"Violet!" Lady Crabbage called, "come partner me!"

Julia and Nicolas also went to play cards, leaving Brynnde to find a seat on a sofa and pick up one of the books on the side table. Sir Everret and Master Collins retired to a corner in which they discussed serious matters in low tones—or at least Brynnde assumed they were serious based on their expressions. Perhaps they were discussing Oliver's curriculum and general lack of discipline.

She was just beginning to read when she became aware of someone standing behind her. Looking up, she discovered Garrick craning to read over her shoulder. She snapped the book shut.

"I was just coming to the best part," Garrick said.

"You should read more quickly," Brynnde told him. "Or better yet find your own book."

He came around the sofa and took a seat on the couch opposite. "No toga this evening?"

"I'm sure I could not come to dinner wrapped in a blanket."

"But you will not catch chill?" Garrick asked.

Brynnde opened her mouth to make some snappish reply but came up short when she noticed the seemingly genuine concern on Garrick's face. "It is only Dr. Shepherd being cautious," she said. Her gaze traveled to the windows made dusky with twilight. "I'm sure he will allow Nicolas and I to go home soon."

Garrick's brows rose. "But I thought you wanted your brother and my sister to make a match. If you leave…"

"And I thought you said there was no chance of it, so why prolong the pain? They are already enthralled," said Brynnde with a nod at the card table. Julia and Nicolas were both laughing over some trick they'd played. "If they continue like this, it will only hurt more when they are forced to part."

"My, my, you *are* morose," Garrick remarked. "Has sitting next to Master Collins brought your spirits low? Or were you thinking he might be better than Mr. Dallweather?"

All the breath went out of Brynnde and she rose, the book tumbling from her lap to the floor. She trembled all over, and for a moment she thought her legs might give way beneath her, but somehow she managed to get out of the parlour, though it seemed she could not see anything in front of her. She was at the foot of the stairs, clinging to the bannister and wondering whether she could make it to her room, when Garrick came after her and took her arm.

"I am sorry, Miss Archambault, no, you must listen to me," he said as Brynnde tried blindly to push him away. "I cannot understand what made me say such a thing. Certainly, I... But please, let me help you..."

Brynnde finally succeeded in wrenching her arm free of his grasp. "You claimed in your note that you wished to remain friends," she said, gathering her dignity and looking him in the eye. "We are not friends, sir. Nor perhaps have we ever been."

And though it took all her might and the full support of the bannister, she walked up the stairs with a rigid spine, aware of iron eyes following her the entire way.

21

———

The next morning Brynnde awakened to a certain amount of hustle and bustle. She could hear footsteps rushing up and down the corridor, but just as she tried to get up and dressed, Dr. Shepherd was shown in. A kindly man with a salt-and-pepper moustache, he declared himself pleased with Brynnde's progress and told her she could sit outdoors so long as she stayed in the sun, muffled up and out of any crosswind.

"No exertion," he told her, wagging his finger. And to a hovering Molly, he said, "No excitement, eh?"

Molly pressed her lips together and nodded. After the doctor had gone, she said, "Perhaps it would be better for you to stay in bed, Miss?"

Brynnde took in Molly's apprehensive expression and knew something was wrong. "What is it, Molly? Why don't you want me to get out of bed?"

"The doctor, he said—"

"Sitting in the parlour or the garden is hardly exciting," Brynnde said preemptively. "What's going on?"

Molly looked over her shoulder at the bedroom door as

if hoping someone would interrupt them. "It's not my place, Miss."

"Oh, Molly, you know better than that. I've never stood on ceremony with you. I've told you everything, and I trust you feel you can do the same. Don't you?" A terrible thought struck Brynnde. "Are you—in trouble?" She would demand Geoffrey's head if he'd compromised Molly.

But Molly blanched, eyes wide at the suggestion. "Oh, no, Miss! It's nothing to do with me!"

Brynnde's mouth went dry. "Who then?"

Voices rose outside the door and a knock sounded. With obvious relief, Molly went to answer it. Garrick stood framed in the doorway, blazing like an avenging angel. Violet hovered behind him, her fists held at her mouth, every line of her signaling distress.

Brynnde all but sprang from the bed; only the knowledge that she was in her nightclothes stopped her. "What?" she asked. "What is it?"

Garrick stepped forward and handed Brynnde a note covered in Julia's untidy scrawl.

I know this must seem sudden—or maybe it doesn't at all— but we couldn't wait through another Season nor risk refusal by our fathers. Wish us happy and when next we meet I shall be Mrs. Archambault!

Julia

BRYNNDE HAD to read it three times before understanding sank in. "They've eloped!"

"So it would seem," Garrick replied grimly. "Though the ride to Scotland is a long one. I may yet be able to catch them."

"You're going after them?" Brynnde asked.

Garrick's fair brows lowered in equal parts determination and confusion. "Of course."

"I suppose my brother is not good enough for your sister," said Brynnde bitterly, not caring who heard.

"Nothing of the sort," said Garrick. "But my family cannot—"

He broke off as a footman hurried up and executed a neat bow. "Your horse is ready, my lord."

Garrick nodded then turned back to Brynnde. "Do not say anything yet to our families. If I can catch them, we may save everyone some anguish."

"Everyone but Nicolas and Julia!" Brynnde cried.

Garrick threw her an exasperated look. "Last night you told me they could not be married and better to separate them!"

"Only because *you* told me it was untenable for them to marry!"

"Oh, and my eloquent argument changed your mind, did it?"

Brynnde threw her hands up. "And I suppose my idea of promoting the match won you over? Yet now you are determined to scotch it!"

Garrick shook his head as though to clear it. "This is getting us nowhere. Clearly, it does not matter what we think or plan. They have made their own decision."

"And you will unmake it," muttered Brynnde.

"I will make them see sense is all," said Garrick. "Give me three days. If I have not overtaken them by then..." He shook his head again. "I must go." He turned and disappeared, leaving both Molly and Violet staring after him.

Brynnde looked again at the note she still held. "I'd be happy for them, if I weren't so infuriated." She threw back the bed covers. "Molly, did Nicolas leave any clothes behind?"

The maid's eyes went round with a mixture of surprise and confusion. "Miss?"

"I can ride faster astride," Brynnde said. "Go look."

Molly exchanged a startled glance with the hovering Violet but bustled off without protest, leaving Violet to say, "But surely you should stay in bed. Dr. Shepherd—"

"No excitement, I know, but it's hardly my fault if others make a to-do." Brynnde went to the dressing table and began to brush and pin her hair. "Tell me everything that's happened this morning."

Violet obliged, telling how she, her mother, and Lord Burbridge had been down at breakfast when Julia's maid came rushing in waving the note. At almost the same time, Dr. Shepherd arrived to check on Brynnde. He also gave Lady Crabbage smelling salts as that lady seemed close to fainting after the news of Julia and Nicolas' flight.

"She blames herself, you see," Violet said, twisting her hands. "Nicolas and Julia remained in the parlour until late, and Mama went to bed."

"She left them alone?" Brynnde gasped.

"Oh no! Mama would never! Master Collins was still there, reading in the corner. He professes to have stayed until they went to bed and followed them upstairs. They were never alone."

"But he did not overhear their conversation," Brynnde guessed.

"It would have been rude to eavesdrop," said Violet.

Brynnde sighed. Violet was right, but she could wish Master Collins had a bit more curiosity than courtesy.

Molly returned then with a handful of clothing Brynnde recognized as her brother's. "Really, Miss," she said, the bundle trembling in her hands, "I'm sure Lord Burbridge can manage, and you should not risk your health."

Brynnde took the clothes and tamped down her impatience; Molly and Violet only wanted her to be well and could not understand her need to act. "I promise to take care of myself," she said. "I suppose Nicolas took his own horse? Violet, is there one I can ride?"

Violet grimaced. "We have a two mares, very gentle..."

Not at all what Brynnde needed. She only just prevented herself stamping her foot in irritation.

"And Oliver has a horse that is the very devil," Violet went on. "But you wouldn't want him..."

"That's perfect," said Brynnde. "Do you think Oliver would let me ride him?"

"Oliver refuses to ride him, so I cannot see why he would mind if someone else did," said Violet. She chewed her lip uncertainly. "The horse is named Bettino. He really is a foul-tempered thing. Oliver may not mind you riding him, but Bettino may have other ideas."

"I don't see I have much choice," Brynnde said. "The mares sound too slow for my purpose. Molly, go see if Bettino can be saddled—*not* a sidesaddle, mind—and made ready. And maybe the kitchen can pack a small provision for me? Quickly, now!" she added when the maid moved reluctantly—and slowly—toward the door.

Brynnde turned to Violet. "Please tell your parents how sorry I am for all the trouble. My illness, my brother, and now I'm sure I'm behaving most improperly, but I really cannot sit and wait for news."

To Brynnde's surprise, Violet smiled a little. "Mama will find it all very exciting. She'll have the grandest story to tell!" Her expression became sober once more. "But we will not say anything for the first few days. If you and Lord Burbridge manage to find them and bring them home…"

"Yes, thank you," said Brynnde. She began laying out the heap of clothing. "Oh, good, a coat." She looked at Violet. The question had to be asked. "Will your mother be able to keep it to herself?"

Violet's mouth became a firm, set line. "I will see to it."

Brynnde gave her friend a quick hug. "And now, if you'll just leave me to dress…"

"Of course." Violet went to the door.

"And see that Burbridge does not leave without me."

Violet gave a resolute nod and was gone.

Minutes later, Brynnde strode down to the entrance hall. If the butler was surprised to see her dressed as a man, he was trained well enough not to show it. He opened the front door and Brynnde stepped out into the September sunshine. The fine weather was holding, but the morning air held a chill to remind everyone summer had ended. Brynnde breathed another small thanks for Nicolas' discarded coat.

Garrick sat on his blood bay. A groom held a second horse, a dark chestnut that pawed the ground and pulled at the reins in the groom's hand. "*Who* told you?" Garrick was asking.

"I dunno, sir, just word from the hou—" The groom stammered to a stop as Brynnde emerged.

"It's for me," Brynnde told Garrick. She turned to the groom. "This is Bettino?"

"Yes'm," said the groom. He did not have the manners the Lowlea butler had shown, and his eyes were wide with astonishment at the sight of Brynnde in her brother's breeches.

No less so than Garrick's, however, whose mouth hung slightly open. Then it snapped shut. "You cannot come with me."

"Then I'll go alone." Brynnde waved away a second groom who had stepped forward to help her into the saddle. Using the step, she swung astride easily. Bettino danced where he stood, and Brynnde patted him, murmuring soothingly.

"Absolutely not!" said Garrick. "The doctor said—"

"My health is none of your concern," Brynnde told him. "And the longer we argue, the closer my brother and your sister get to Scotland."

"You'd be pleased if they got there," Garrick accused.

Brynnde smiled. "But I'd hate to miss the wedding."

A housemaid ran out with some wrapped sandwiches, though she hesitated when she saw Bettino. One of the grooms accepted the sandwiches instead and put them in Brynnde's saddlebag.

Brynnde watched Garrick master himself, the way he clinched the reins and pressed his lips together, expelling air through his nostrils much like Bettino was doing. Garrick fought himself; Brynnde saw the mental argument taking place behind the thundercloud eyes. She held her breath until Garrick's shoulders relaxed in resignation. The need for speed had won out.

"Are you certain you can handle him?" Garrick asked, nodding at Bettino.

"I've managed my share of difficult beasts," said Brynnde. She took the reins and the groom stepped away as Garrick wheeled his bay around.

"Keep up," he said and was off with Brynnde close behind.

HOW FAR COULD *they have gotten?* Brynnde wondered as they rode. They'd stopped at every likely inn, every place where horses might be changed. At one such place Brynnde identified Nicolas' blue roan, and they were told that yes, a young man and his missus had come through and boarded the horse, promising to be back for it in a couple days. They'd hired another horse and gone on.

"When was this?" Garrick demanded.

"Early this morning, like," the stable lad answered. "Too early even for breakfast, it was. They must've been in some hurry, hey?" He eyed them with undisguised curiosity, his gaze going again and again to Brynnde in her brother's clothes.

"Yes, they must," said Garrick grimly.

"They will have to stop some time," Brynnde said as they rode on. "They have to eat!"

"So do we. And sleep." Garrick grimaced. "We *must* reach them before the news can spread."

"They are clearly already posing as husband and wife," said Brynnde, remembering what the stable boy had said.

"Which means they will ask for only one room if and when they stop for the night," said Garrick. He shook his head. "What a disaster."

"Is it?" Brynnde asked, musing aloud. "Nicolas and Julia married and happy together does not seem so terrible to me."

Garrick sighed. "This again. It isn't that I begrudge their happiness, or even condemn a possible future union between them. Heaven knows, I—" He bit back whatever he'd been about to say and changed direction. "But right now things are so tenuous for my family, what with Graeme's misstep and Eleanor marrying a merchant..." He shook his head again, and Brynnde was momentarily distracted by the way it absorbed the daylight, as though his hair were itself made of spun sunbeams.

His next words broke the spell. "We cannot tolerate another blow such as this."

"Your father is an earl!" Brynnde cried. "He will not lose his title over any of this! Gossip will not harm him, or you—any of you! But you would rather see your own brother and sisters unhappy than be touched by rumors."

Garrick looked over at her, eyes blazing and face sharp in its seriousness. "Scandal *can* harm us. It can isolate us. We would be unable to sustain ourselves socially if others chose to cut us. One small thing like Graeme we could bury in the country. Eleanor marrying Thomas Dryer, well, let us just say I was not for the match. At the very least, I felt she should wait. And if Julia elopes? We will be known far and wide for being wayward and unconventional, a whole generation of improper, unreliable—"

"Then go! Travel! Isn't that what you prefer to do anyway? You needn't be any part of what happens here."

"I will some day be the Earl of Darley," said Garrick. "All that my siblings do reflects on me and the family name. No matter where I travel, this is what I will return to."

With that, he spurred his horse to greater speed and the ability to converse was lost. Brynnde kept pace without trouble; Bettino had tried early on to go his own way, but Brynnde's firm hand soon had him obeying.

Under other circumstances, Brynnde would have found the autumn countryside charming. The trees were turning from green to copper and gold, and they occasionally passed ponds where ducks sailed placidly on the dark surface of the water. Alas, at speed there was no time to indulge in the view.

They continued on in silence until a high layer of clouds rolled in and the light faded. With night coming on, they were forced to stop. And none too soon, in Brynnde's opinion; the wind was beginning to increase and she smelled moisture in the air.

Garrick voiced her thoughts. "Rain," he said as they reined in at the stable yard of an inn. His eyes ran over Brynnde and she shivered, though she assured herself it was due to the chill air. "You cannot afford to be caught out in the damp," he said.

"And you cannot leave me here alone!" Brynnde countered.

"Of course not," he sighed, though his gaze continually ventured back to the road. "They will have to stop, too. We must simply start earlier in the morning than they do so as to overcome the distance between us."

They dismounted, gave the horses over to the grooms, and entered the warmth of the inn whose sign proclaimed it to be The Crowned Lion. It looked much like all the others they'd seen that day, and as with everywhere they'd stopped, people ceased talking and stared as they came in. "Speaking of reputation," Garrick muttered.

"You are worried word will get out that Lord Burbridge has been seen riding all over the countryside with a woman in men's clothing?"

"My concern is more for you than me. No one is likely to know us here, but to be safe, let's not use our names." Garrick greeted the innkeeper while Brynnde hung back. Suddenly her usual indifference to others' opinions seemed to have fled. She became very aware of the two dozen eyes on her.

"My sister and I would like rooms for the evening," Garrick said. When the man only gawped, Garrick snapped his fingers. "Two rooms," he said. "And a meal."

The innkeeper—short and with hair in all the wrong places—grunted. "And will you be needing the coach, too?"

"What?" Garrick asked sharply.

"Ain't no big houses out here, no fancy visitors. Don't normally get gentry 'cept on the way to Gretna. Youse running off with the mistress, eh?"

Brynnde saw from the way Garrick's brows lowered and fists clinched on the polished wood that he might grab the man and pull him over the counter. She stepped up quickly, not sorry for the added security of being closer to Garrick. "Has anyone else come through recently? On the way to Gretna Green?"

The innkeeper looked her over in a way she didn't much like. "They said they was already married, but no newly-weds coming out this way, 'cept when coming *back* from Gretna. Coach goes direct there. Good business in it. We can keep your horses for you."

Garrick and Brynnde exchanged glances. "When did the coach leave?" Garrick asked.

"Just missed the last one by ten minutes. Won't be another 'til morning."

"And this couple was on it?" Brynnde asked breathlessly.

Now the innkeeper cocked a suspicious eye at her. "What's your int'rest? Weren't no kidnapping. Two of them happy as birds in a tree."

Garrick turned to Brynnde. "I have to try and catch up to that coach."

"Then I'm coming with you."

"It's getting cold out, and dark, and the rain will start any minute."

"So?" Brynnde asked.

But Garrick had already turned back to the innkeeper. "A room for her, and dinner. And I'll need a fresh horse."

"Garrick Sommerford, if you leave me here, I will tell the whole of Christendom that you abandoned me after spending a day alone in my company!" Brynnde hissed.

Garrick stared at her a moment. "You wouldn't," he finally said.

Brynnde's eyebrows went up, challenging him to try it.

Mouth set in a grim line, Garrick turned to the innkeeper once more.

"Two fresh horses," he said.

22

———

The rain came hard and cold, blowing nearly sideways in the gusts of wind. The horses from the inn had the benefit of being rested but Brynnde struggled with hers, which appeared determined to turn back and go home. She could hardly blame him; more than once she wondered whether she should have stayed at The Crowned Lion after all.

The weather made it impossible to converse. Brynnde bent low in her saddle and squinted through the gloom to keep Garrick in her sights. His dark, wet clothing was lost in the blackness, but his bright hair served as beacon enough.

Brynnde reminded herself that if they were struggling to travel, so must the coach be, and so there remained the chance of catching up to it. She did not know what she hoped for after that. To convince Garrick to allow the elopement? After all the trouble of finding their siblings, it seemed unlikely he would agree.

And perhaps Garrick was right. Nicolas and Julia could wait a few months, even until next Season, and have a proper wedding. By then Graeme and even Eleanor would be established and fading from society's memories. No reason to rush.

The memory of Julia's ecstatic face swam into Brynnde's mind. Love, it seemed, demanded immediate action. Love did not like to wait.

And Nicolas, usually so staid... Clearly he felt the same urgency.

Brynnde shivered and hunched further against the driving rain. She had felt no such drive to marry Garrick, though no aversion to the idea either. But certainly it could not be love between them, else they too would have been spurred to run away.

Ahead of her, Garrick began to slow. Brynnde followed suit and brought her horse alongside his. She could barely make out what had caused him to drop to a walk, but as they grew nearer she distinguished the heaping shape of the coach pulled partially off the road. It appeared to have missed a turn and ended up stuck in the mud on the verges, and the lanterns had gone out. The horses hung their heads in the downpour, a sad sight. The driver was nowhere to be seen.

Garrick motioned for Brynnde to stop as he drew up his horse beside the coach and rapped at the door. Without receiving any response that Brynnde could see, he then pulled open the door. Brynnde craned to one side, even going so far as to bring her horse a few steps to the left for a better look, but it was useless, too dark to see.

The coach was occupied, that much was clear as Garrick held a quick conversation with the occupants. He then waved Brynnde over. "Climb inside!" he called over the roar of the rain.

Brynnde dismounted, practically sliding off the saddle, and tied her horse to the back of the coach. Her legs felt frozen through, and even the few steps to the coach door were an effort. She leaned around to look inside, but before she could distinguish anything concrete in the darkness, a familiar voice squealed, "Brynnde!" Hands pulled her inside and established her on the bench.

"Julia," Brynnde said through chattering teeth.

"You shouldn't be out in this," Nicolas' voice said from the opposite corner. Brynnde squinted to try and see him but could only make out vague patches where his white shirt was visible under his waistcoat and coat.

Before Brynnde could respond, Garrick clambered in and took the seat across from her. "Neither should you be," he said as he pulled the door shut. "Julia, this is the second time you've put Miss Archambault in danger of her health."

"Well, I hardly expected her to come after us!" Julia cried. Brynnde sensed rather than saw Julia turn toward her. "Why would you try to stop us?"

"I don't want to stop you," Brynnde said, though forming words proved difficult. Her jaw seemed locked due to the cold. "If anything, I would happily bear witness to the event. But Ga—Lord Burbridge, that is, worries it would be one too many blows to the family name."

She could feel Garrick's scowl from across the coach. Yet all he said was, "Where is the driver?"

"Gone for help," said Nicolas.

"And leaving you two alone," Garrick added, his voice tight.

"Well, then, we will have to get married now!" said Julia.

"We will get you back to Lowlea and pretend none of this ever happened," Garrick told her. "No one need know."

Brynnde wanted to argue the cause, but chills wracked her body, making it impossible to speak. She felt Julia move beside her then the warmth of a traveling cloak fell over her shoulders. Julia's words were oddly muffled when she spoke. "Garrick, how could you think of bringing her out in this?"

"She gave me no choice," Garrick protested.

"You could have both stayed at Lowlea," Julia countered.

The warmth of the cloak, while welcome, created a miasma of damp heat around Brynnde. She began to cough as well as shake.

Garrick leaned toward the coach window. "Where is that damned driver?"

"Garrick!" Julia gasped.

He only sniffed. "You pretend not to know such words, but I've heard you use them yourself."

"Yes, but I'm not the only lady present," Julia reminded him.

"Oh, Bryn knows and uses those words, too," said Nicolas.

Brynnde thought of some choice words for him but her jaw had firmly clamped itself shut in defense against the bone-rattling tremors.

Someone drew the cloak tighter around her. Julia? But it was Garrick who spoke. "We need to get her somewhere warm and dry."

"Bryn?" Nicolas asked, but his voice sounded far away to Brynnde's ears. Brynnde swayed where she sat. Gray spots danced behind her eyes. There was motion, and Garrick said, "No, I've got her."

Strong arms gathered Brynnde up and she felt the additional warmth of another body close to hers. She was vaguely aware of being held, possibly on a lap. Her head lolled against a damp shoulder.

"Stupid girl," Garrick murmured in her ear. "Should have stayed at the inn."

There came the faint sound of voices outside the coach.

"Here now, what's this? Where did these horses—oh, but they're from the inn!"

"The driver." Even as Nicolas said it, the coach door opened. Brynnde opened her eyes a fraction and saw the rectangle of slightly less dark and the silhouette of a squat man in a tall hat.

"Picked up a couple more, did we?" the man asked.

"This, sir, is my sister," said Garrick.

"She ill?" asked the man.

"What? No, not this one—" Brynnde felt herself lifted an inch or two in exhibit. "That one. I insist that you bring her, and all of us, back to the inn from which you left."

"Wedding been called off, has it?" the man asked.

"Yes," said Garrick.

"No," said Julia.

Brynnde saw the man's head move as he looked from one to the other of them. "Which is it?"

A pause. Then Nicolas' voice came low and clear. "No."

A surge of pride warmed Brynnde. Good for Nicolas, standing up for what he wanted. She was sure Julia appreciated it, too. She lifted her head a little and croaked, "No."

"Seems you're outnumbered," the man said.

"Yes, but my word counts for more than all three of theirs combined," said Garrick. "Turn this coach around and take us back to The Crowned Lion."

The man pursed his lips and nodded as though in thought. Then a voice called from somewhere outside the coach, "Hoy, Jacob, we can't move it with these horses tied here!"

Garrick shifted beneath Brynnde, and she realized with regret that he was moving to put her down. The loss of his body heat was immediate and unwelcome.

"Mr. Archambault, if you would?" Garrick asked.

The bench felt hard after Garrick's lap, and it required Brynnde's reserves of strength to stay sitting upright as he and Nicolas exited the coach. Across from her, Brynnde sensed Julia lean forward. "You really aren't well," she said, her tone tight with concern.

"I will be fine," Brynnde insisted, though she suspected the words came out more mumbled than she intended. "You must take your cloak back."

"No!" said Julia. "You need it far more than I do."

Brynnde shook her head and the darkness swam around her like black water threatening to drown her. "You must take it and the horses and go."

"The horses?" Julia asked.

"From the inn. Quickly, before Garrick mounts and ruins everything." Brynnde fumbled with the cloak, trying to remove it, but her fingers refused to obey.

"You really think so? We should run away? Again?"

"You made it this far," said Brynnde. "I'll do what I can to stall him, or else talk sense into him."

"Well, he won't leave you to chase us," Julia said. "Not in the state your in."

Brynnde wished she were as confident about that. Then again, Garrick had held her on his lap. And Nicolas hadn't even tried to stop him! Brynnde tried to give her brother the benefit of the doubt—maybe he'd been unable to see what was happening.

Finally succeeding in freeing herself of the cloak, Brynnde shoved it at her friend. "Go!"

Julia did not have to be told twice. Pausing only to kiss Brynnde's cheek and breathe, "Thank you!" she darted out of the coach. Brynnde noted when the door opened that the rain had slowed to a patter.

Brynnde had almost drifted off when Garrick appeared at the open coach door. "Miss Archambault!"

With effort, Brynnde opened her eyes.

"My sister—"

"I know. I told her to go," Brynnde mumbled. Her eyes closed again. Her entire body felt too heavy.

"What?" Garrick asked. "Julia told me you had taken a turn for the worse. We must get you back to the inn…"

The sound of horses passing the coach prompted Brynnde to struggle upright. "Oh," she said. "You must have already been on the horse."

Garrick was looking over his shoulder at the riders. "What the devil?" His head snapped 'round and his fierce gaze landed on Brynnde. "You're behind this?"

"I only told her they should take the horses the rest of the way to Gretna Green." A fit of coughing overcame Brynnde.

"And Julia conspired to get me off my horse by telling me you were gravely ill. And I fell for it." He eyed Brynnde's hunched figure. "You can stop pretending. They're well gone."

Brynnde did not, could not move. Her last reserves of energy had been used up in clearing the way for Julia and Nicolas. The damp clothes stuck to her, the coat so heavy with water she could not lift her arms, the rest too insubstantial to hold in any heat. She only wanted to lie down and sleep for a week. Again.

Indeed, she was slipping sideways where she sat when Garrick jumped into the coach to right her. "Or perhaps Julia was not lying. How kind of her to leave her dear, sick friend to pursue her own pleasure."

Brynnde wanted to tell him not to be too hard on Julia, that she—Brynnde—had insisted that Julia go. But even her cheeks felt like stone, unable to move. She found herself slumped against Garrick's side and helpless to do anything about it. Not that she was sure she wanted to. He was warm at least.

Then, amidst shouts and grunts from outside, the coach shifted beneath them. Garrick gathered Brynnde closer to him as the men maneuvered the coach back onto the road.

"Are you all right?" he asked once everything became still.

"Mm," was all Brynnde could manage.

Brynnde watched through half-open eyes as Jacob, the driver, stuck his head in through the open door. "Wedding on again, is it? Will we be joining the party, or—?"

"No," Garrick snapped, and Brynnde felt his growl reverberate through his body. "Can't you see she's ill? We must get back to the inn and find a doctor."

Jacob touched his hat. "Yessir. Yours is the words that count, after all." He closed the door and moments later the coach was turning around.

"We'll get you someplace warm and dry," Garrick promised.

"You'll let them go?" Brynnde asked thickly, her lips not wanting to comply.

Garrick leaned in close. "Is that really all that matters to you?"

"I only want them to be happy," Brynnde told him.

He sighed. "If their being happy will make you happy..."

"I want you to be happy too," said Brynnde. "Why?" she murmured, her thoughts foggy as exhaustion crept in; she did not even know she was speaking aloud. "Why can't you be happy for them?"

If there were any answer, Brynnde was asleep before she could hear it.

23

———

She was hot, she was cold. Her skin felt damp and clammy but her mouth parched. She could not get comfortable and yet her limbs were too heavy to rearrange into better position. So it went for Brynnde knew not how long.

At last she woke to the sight of an unnaturally grizzled face peering at her from above. It took her a moment to recognize it.

It was clear Garrick had not shaved in a number of days, nor trimmed what had grown. His already prominent cheekbones were all the more so in the thinning face, which made his eyes appear larger as well. Those stormy orbs were shadowed with lack of sleep, and his tan had faded. His clothes were wrinkled and hung loosely over Garrick's diminishing frame.

"You look terrible," Brynnde croaked.

He only stared at her, and for a minute Brynnde thought he might be asleep with his eyes open. But then he blinked in a way that suggested someone fighting back tears. "Thank you," he said.

He turned his head then, and Brynnde followed his gaze to the small window that only allowed the most persistent rays of sunlight to penetrate the glass. It was a plain room but made cozy by a fire in the grate. The Crowned Lion, Brynnde remembered suddenly, and the rest began to flood back as well. Julia and Nicolas! She turned back to Garrick, prepared to demand answers as to what had happened, but he held up a hand.

"Yes, they made it to Gretna Green and are happily married," he told her.

"Are they here?" Brynnde asked. She struggled to sit up but it was no use; she had no strength and collapsed back to her pillow.

Garrick blinked and shook his head like a man just waking up. "You need water, and some bread and broth," he said, rising. "I'll be back shortly." Brynnde noticed his legs were stiff and steps unsteady as he left.

Once his footsteps faded, Brynnde tried again to sit up, but the best she could manage was to slide her back up the pillow a little way. Her neck felt hardly strong enough to hold her head. She wondered how long she'd been at the inn and who else might be there. Why hadn't Garrick answered her when she'd asked about Nicolas and Julia? A dart of anxiety pierced Brynnde's heart. Had something happened to them? Had the families disowned them? But no, she could not imagine her father going so far. He wanted Nicolas to settle down, and though eloping would not have been Papa's first choice—and certainly not Maman's either —he would never be so angry as to turn Nicolas out of his inheritance.

But perhaps Lord Darley had taken it badly? If so, it was no wonder Garrick appeared so grim.

A scuffling sound from outside the door drew Brynnde's

attention away from her thoughts. Garrick entered, awkwardly bearing a laden tray, which he set on the table beside the chair he'd been sitting in earlier. The smell of the broth caused Brynnde's stomach to gurgle with anticipation; she was sure Garrick heard it. She reached for the bowl, but Garrick gave her hand a light slap. "You'll only spill it all over yourself," he said. "Let me."

First, he came to the side of the bed and lifted Brynnde gently forward so he could set the pillows at a better angle. She rested back against them, finally able to sit up. When she reached again for the broth, Garrick said, "Ah-ah," as though reprimanding a child. He picked up the spoon, dipped it into the bowl and held it out to her.

Brynnde drew away, though it nearly caused her to topple sideways. "You can't be serious."

"I can be and I am," said Garrick. "You can barely lift your arms much less feed yourself. Come now. You need to rebuild your strength."

Brynnde scowled but the smell of the broth was too tempting to refuse. Reluctantly, she leaned forward and allowed Garrick to slip the spoon into her mouth. The broth was hot and savory and warmed her straight down to her toes.

After a few more bites, Brynnde asked, "Where is Molly? If anyone should be doing this—and I don't admit it needs doing—it should be her, not you."

Garrick grimaced and set the bowl aside. "There is not enough room here for everyone to stay, and you have been in no need of a maid."

"Who *is* here then?" Brynnde asked.

"At first it was a relative parade of people," Garrick told her. "We took up every room here and several in other inns some miles away. But, of course, business could not be suspended indefinitely..." His voice became bitter. "The physician comes daily and the rector sends 'round what I am sure he thinks of as kind notes..."

"Papa?" Brynnde asked faintly. Surely at least her father was there!

Garrick smiled, though it was strained. "He is in the process of turning Aux Arbres over to your brother and moving your mother and sister to the townhouse in London. I will send for him directly. He will be beyond relieved to hear you are awake."

"No one... No one else stayed?" Brynnde asked. "How—how long...?"

Garrick shook his head. "I've lost track," he said with a small frown of concentration. "Two weeks, or three... Not a month yet, I don't think." His slate eyes met hers. "No one wanted to abandon you, Br—Miss Archambault. But as there was nothing to be done, it made no sense for everyone to stay. Here," he said, rising again, "I have quite the collection of letters from everyone asking for news of you. I will go fetch it and you can read for yourself everyone's care and concern."

He left again and returned moments later with a thick stack of envelopes. The two of them spent no little time laughing over Julia's remarks about having been married first, and how everyone should elope as the wedding preparations at Ridgemow had become increasingly chaotic. Julia was there to help as the big day drew near but wished to be either at Brynnde's bedside—"though I can't do more than you, Garrick, and probably would do less"—or installing herself at Aux Arbres. *Just married and already separated! But only until Graeme and Ellie are married. Nicolas will come for the weddings, and I will return to Aux Arbres with him.*

The letters from Violet were earnest and tearful. *I should have insisted that she stay and follow Dr. Shepherd's orders!* Brynnde remembered her promise to bring Violet back to Aux Arbres so she may further her acquaintance with Mr. Dallweather and felt terrible for failing her friend. Would she still have the opportunity to do so once she was well enough to travel?

Letters from both Lord Averland and Lady Darley pressed Garrick to write with any news of Brynnde's condition. Then Garrick slipped past one in the stack that had Lady Averland's handwriting on it.

"What about that one?" Brynnde asked, reaching for it.

"More of the same," Garrick said, but his tone belied the nonchalance of the words.

Brynnde reached out and snatched the envelope, turning away from Garrick when he attempted to take it back. She gasped when she read it.

"That bad?" Brynnde whispered.

Her mother had written to ask Garrick whether she should begin dying some garments black and having scarfs and gloves made.

"Points for practicality," Garrick muttered, pulling the page from Brynnde's hands and standing again. "I will go write to everyone forthwith unless you need anything?"

Brynnde shook her head, too stunned by her mother's letter to say anything.

"Get some rest," said Garrick. "The physician will be here before long."

Brynnde couldn't imagine being able to sleep, though between the warmth of the fire and her now full belly, she did feel content. She must have drifted off, for she awakened to the door opening and a very round man with a bristly moustache entering the room.

"Well, well," he said, "We're awake, are we?"

Brynnde wondered whether perhaps she was *not* awake and, in fact, dreaming.

"I'm Dr. Davies," the man went on. "You must have a strong will, Miss Archambault. Or *he* does." The physician began his rudimentary examination, and only then did Brynnde realize she was wearing one of her nightdresses. Someone must have brought it and—her cheeks heated at the thought—dressed her. Molly, she hoped. Yes, almost certainly Molly.

Brynnde cleared her throat. "Please, can you tell me how long I've been here?"

"Eighteen days," said Dr. Davies.

"It must be November," Brynnde realized.

"The second," Dr. Davies told her.

The double wedding was set for the fifteenth. "Will I be able to travel soon?" Brynnde asked.

"Let's not rush things." The physician finished his examination and seemed satisfied as he gathered himself to leave. "As I understand it, rushing is what landed you here in the first place, hmm? I'll be back tomorrow and we'll see how you're improving—*if* you're improving. Lots of fluids now, and keep wrapped up."

Brynnde groaned. She didn't even have a book to keep herself occupied! Maybe she could write some letters of her own. She looked around for a bell but there wasn't one. She tossed herself back onto her pillows in exasperation, wondering whether to try getting out of bed but not at all certain her legs would hold her up. She resigned herself to wait.

It wasn't long. Garrick returned a few minutes later looking much more his usual self—shaved and in clean, neat clothing, though the clothes hung a tad more loosely than before. Brynnde wondered whether Geoffrey was in attendance somewhere.

Brynnde asked Garrick for writing utensils, and he quickly supplied them. She wrote a letter to Violet pledging to bring her to Aux Arbres as soon as possible and apologizing for the long wait, for being silly headed enough to go after Nicolas and Julia. She penned a missive to Julia, too, regretting that she might have to miss the double wedding at Ridgemow, a property she longed to see, though the idea she might have become its mistress made the prospect bittersweet.

It occurred to Brynnde that Garrick would have to return to Ridgemow regardless of her own health and ability to travel. That he'd stayed while everyone else returned to their lives said something, though Brynnde could not think clearly enough to figure out what. She was tired despite all the bed rest; her body felt exhausted after the simple work of writing.

Garrick had excused himself with the promise of returning later with her dinner, and this he did, this time with a tray set for two. He pulled the small table between them and asked, "Are you all right to feed yourself?"

"If I can hold a pen, I can hold a spoon," Brynnde told him.

"Don't overextend yourself," Garrick warned. "You spent so much energy on the pen you might not have any for the spoon."

Brynnde could not deny his logic and took it slow, enjoying the simple but flavorful broth and fresh bread. She eyed the bit of rabbit on Garrick's plate and he offered her a bite. "Not too much now," he said. "You can't tolerate solid food in quantity yet."

"You sound like Molly," Brynnde said as she swallowed the tasty morsel.

Garrick sat back against the chair, evidently finished with his meal. "Your family will be coming as soon as they receive my letters, I daresay."

"And then you will be free to return to Ridgemow to finish preparations for the weddings!" Brynnde tried to smile and sound cheerful about it though deep down she wished she could go too. How she longed to see Julia and Eleanor! To hear all about Gretna Green! Well, that day would come. She only had to wait and do as the doctor said this time.

Brynnde became aware of Garrick's narrowed gaze. "It sounds as though you will be moving to London with your parents and sister," he said, his tone loose and idle as though only discussing the weather.

But to Brynnde it felt like a poked bruise. She tried but could not fully hold up her smile. "Yes, I suppose so." She hadn't considered that. And it meant not being able to invite Violet to spend time with Mr. Dallweather either. She would fail her friend.

Garrick's eyes remained fixed on her. "What worries you?" he asked, and the gentleness in his tone crept under Brynnde's skin and crawled beneath it in a way that made tears prick at her eyes. Why was he being so nice?

Brynnde blinked away the intrusive tears. "Nothing. Or... Everything, perhaps. I don't know."

"Mr. Dallweather?" Garrick suggested. "If you marry him, you will be able to stay near Aux Arbres, near your brother and Julia."

Brynnde's heart froze in her chest. Suddenly Garrick did not seem nice at all. "You think I should marry Mr. Dall-weather?" she asked.

"I am only helping you consider your options. If you do not wish to move to London—"

"I have nothing against London, though I will miss the countryside," said Brynnde. "It is only that I promised Violet another stay at Aux Arbres so that she could... That is, she and Mr. Dallweather..."

"Ah. Matchmaking again," Garrick said.

"You assume that because I could not find someone else for myself I must now be looking for someone else for Mr. Dallweather!" cried Brynnde. "But I assure you they suit. They met only briefly, but if you could have seen them—"

She broke off when Garrick stood up and came to sit on the side of her bed. "What—?"

But Garrick took her hands in his. "I see no obstacles now to us renewing our engagement."

Brynnde pulled her hands away. "Oh, so *now* it is convenient? Well, I hardly need the favor *now* so long as I can get Violet and Mr. Dallweather in the same room. They can do the rest on their own."

"They could both attend our wedding," Garrick said reasonably, "and re-form their acquaintance."

Brynnde stared. "Marrying someone just to allow two other people to spend time together is a bit extreme. I'm sure I can convince Julia to throw some kind of party at Aux Arbres that will work just as well."

Garrick sat back, exasperation written over his features. "You are deliberately misunderstanding me," he said.

"And you—" Brynnde clinched her fists and shook her head though it caused the room to spin when she did. "I don't even know what! You insist we cannot be engaged, and then neither can Julia and Nicolas, but now they're happily married despite you, and—and—now you've decided it will be all right for us to be married too?" She threw up her hands. "If this is what I get in our brief moments together, I cannot imagine living a life so infuriating!"

"Better not to imagine it," Garrick agreed, his expression all seriousness. "I would hate for it to disappoint, after all. Then again," he added, eyes twinkling, "you might yet be pleasantly surprised."

Brynnde's mouth hung open. "But don't you understand?" she asked. "You don't have to marry me! I don't need to be rescued from Mr. Dallweather now. I just need to—"

"I know, you just need to match him and Miss Crabbage and all will be well. But did it ever occur to you, Miss Archambault, that I was not attempting to rescue you?"

Brynnde blinked at him.

"That I might actually want to marry you for reasons all my own?" Garrick asked. And when Brynnde still appeared confused, "That I could..." He stopped and cleared his throat. "That I could be in love with you?"

Brynnde stared a minute longer, noted the faint pink along Garrick's cheeks. Then she sat back. "Oh, you're not very nice at all, are you? Teasing a poor, sick girl! Just because you got stuck here looking after me and are bored to tears when you'd rather be traveling the world—"

Garrick stood up. "You have formed some very definite opinions about me, Miss Archambault, and I am sure some of that is my own fault. But I assure you I did not get 'stuck' here. I chose to stay of my own accord. If you would like me to leave, you need only say so." He turned his attention to the tray on the table, gathering utensils so as to take it away.

"No, wait, I..." Brynnde faltered as the thunderstorm eyes found hers. "I'm sorry. I don't know what to say." She ran a palm over her forehead. "Thank you for taking care of me. And for your kind offer."

"But?" Garrick prompted.

Brynnde was confused again. "But what?"

"It sounded as though you were refusing my 'kind offer'."

"Oh. No, not at all," Brynnde said. "I think I love you. Not lightning love like Molly and—Oh! But if we get married then Molly and Geoffrey can be together too! So that's all right."

Garrick put his hands to his head. "I think I'm coming down with something. Nothing makes sense any more." He stopped and looked at her. "Did you say you love me?"

Brynnde nodded. "I think so. Molly says sometimes love is sort of slow, but when you think about someone a lot and wish they were there, that's usually a sign."

"Molly is an expert, is she? Well," Garrick said, "I take heart in the knowledge you at least think of me and wish I were around. It's a start.

"There is just one thing I must know, however, before we can make our betrothal official," he went on, and Brynnde's eyes grew wide with anticipation. What could he want to know that he did not already? And would her answer determine their future?

"Your name," said Garrick. "It is most unusual. Is it a family name? French?"

"You want to know about my name?" Brynnde asked.

"I want to know about *you*. Your name is only one of your many mysteries."

Brynnde shifted where she sat, the bed feeling suddenly lumpy and uncomfortable beneath her.

"You do know something about it!" said Garrick. "Is it such a terrible story?"

"Not really, just... A little embarrassing." The look of genuine concern on his face had Brynnde spilling to him yet again. "When I was born—it was a long and hard labor, I've been assured—my mother called for some brandy after delivering me. But her words were slurred, and the doctor thought she was naming me. He gave the name to our vicar to be recorded and..." She shrugged. "You do have a way of drawing things out of me," she added ruefully.

"Good. I like drawing you out. You're full of the most amazing things, and I cannot wait to spend a lifetime discovering them."

24

___

*B*rynnde's family arrived the following day and Molly was with them. The maid was ecstatic when she heard the news of the re-engagement. Lord Averland, for his part, seemed relieved, and not only to see Brynnde settled. "I had my misgivings in leaving Burbridge here with you," he confided to Brynnde one afternoon. "Not that I believed he would do anything improper, and nor would you, but for appearances..."

That had not occurred to Brynnde. Word would surely get around the inn, the nearby villages, and eventually the wider world. "Then his marrying me is the honorable thing," she murmured.

"Oh, don't start with that now," Garrick told her when he next came in to visit and she voiced her insecurities. "I told you, I want to marry you because I love you. No slow bloom for me. Molly's proverbial lightning struck the first time I saw you."

"But you were so rude!" Brynnde cried.

Garrick's lips twisted wryly. "I do seem to say all the wrong things when in love. Funny, I can court a woman I have no interest in with perfect gallantry, but confront me with someone I truly like, and I step all over myself."

Brynnde laughed. "Then I will only ever worry if I see you making a mess of things around another woman." She sighed contentedly. "I do enjoy that I can tell you anything, no matter how small or foolish it may seem."

Garrick gave her a swift kiss on the forehead. "That is as it should be between two people in love. Now I'm off to Ridgemow and hope to have you there with me shortly." And he was gone.

Dr. Davies relented and gave permission for Brynnde to remove to Ridgemow just two days prior to the planned double—now triple—wedding. "I feel like a Christmas goose!" Brynnde protested from beneath the layers of clothing and rugs tucked around her. She could hardly move for having been stuffed into the pile of fabrics.

"If you're to go at all, it must be like this," her mother told her. Brynnde had no platform from which to object; the last time she had gone against her physician's orders, she had ended up worse off than before. So she resigned herself to being padded and handled like something fragile for the time being.

They arrived at dusk. Brynnde's first impression of her future home was only of a large, square, stone building. Stairs led up to a tall, columned portico that she felt was more forbidding than inviting. But then the door opened and warm light spilled out from the lamp held by the butler who directed the footmen with alacrity. Next thing Brynnde knew, she was inside the biggest entry she had ever seen, and Eleanor and Julia were on either side of her, talking at the same time, laughing, and being generally confusing in the most wonderful way. Brynnde relaxed. These were her sisters now!

The thought caused Brynnde to look for Tessa who remained beside Lady Averland. Tessa's expression was customarily sullen, but in her personal joy Brynnde could afford to be magnanimous. She waved Tessa over. Tessa's expression went from dour to perplexed and wary, but she joined them. It seemed Julia and Eleanor understood, and they went out of their way to include Tessa in the conversation, asking about clothes and discussing what it might be like to live in London. As Tessa thawed her natural beauty began to shine more even than usual, and the less self-conscious she was of that beauty the more likable she became. Brynnde thought, *If only she could be like this all the time! We might have gotten along.* She wondered whether their mother's high expectations had pressured Tessa and turned her hard the way heavy soil did rocks to form gemstones. Perhaps, after she and Garrick were settled, she would invite Tessa to stay. Maybe there was someone nearby who would make an eligible match, or a friend of Graeme's or Garrick's...

"You haven't heard a word I've said!" Julia scolded. "Poor thing, you must be exhausted, and it's almost time for dinner anyway. Here, we'll show you both to your rooms." And so amidst much chatter, they went upstairs to freshen up and change.

"You're scheming again," Garrick said in a low voice as they waited in the drawing room before dinner. Brynnde had been watching Tessa, whose shell had melted under the warmth of Eleanor and Julia. It had never occurred to Brynnde that her sister had just as few—fewer, even— friends than she had. Aux Arbres was lovely, but isolated, and while Brynnde had adapted to that without trouble, a vivacious personality such as Tessa's required more society. London would be good for her.

Brynnde turned to her fiancé. "Only thinking," she said with a smile as the butler announced dinner.

"Just don't let it get you into any more trouble," Garrick warned.

Brynnde was given the seat next to Lady Darley who reached out and squeezed her hand where it rested on the table. "You have no idea how pleased we all are, my dear," she said. Her gaze flicked in the direction of Graeme, who did not miss the censure.

"It all came out for the best," Graeme said.

"You could have saved a lot of people a lot of trouble with a little proper behavior," his mother told him.

Graeme grinned. "But it would not have been half so much fun. And Ellie would not be marrying Mr. Dryer if all had gone according to plan. So there, Ellie, you have me to thank for that."

"Oh, I don't know," said Garrick, "I think Mother and Father would have allowed it eventually."

Brynnde took in the twinkle in Lady Darley's eye and the twist of Lord Darley's lips and knew it to be true.

Julia leaned to get Brynnde's attention from down the table. "Is Miss Crabbage coming to the wedding?"

Brynnde smiled. "Oh, yes! And Mr. Dallweather."

"Dallweather?" Nicolas echoed as he cut his meat. "Why would your suitor come to see you marry another man?"

"He wouldn't marry me now if I came with a pot of gold," said Brynnde. "My having been so ill would definitely put him off me. But Miss Crabbage has quite a resilient constitution. Why, she was the only one of us who did not get sick..." Brynnde's words fell off and she threw a look at Julia.

"Oh, we know all about the fountain," Eleanor said.

"Ridiculous," added Lady Darley, but her eyes were still twinkling. Brynnde suspected she'd played in her share of fountains in her youth.

THE NEXT DAY was consumed by pre-wedding bustle as guests arrived and Brynnde's things, diverted from going to London, also appeared in her bedroom. "No sense unpacking it all, though," said Molly, "seeing as you'll be moving rooms again tomorrow."

Most wonderful of all, Parnassus came, and with him an unexpected friend—Violet had brought Bettino as a wedding gift. "Oliver can't ride him. None of us can. But somehow you were able to, so..."

Brynnde embraced her friend. "I have something for you, too. Or rather, someone."

Violet's brown eyes were wide with apprehension as Brynnde led her into the drawing room where Mr. Dallweather had already affixed himself to a sofa and was reading.

"Miss Crabbage," said Brynnde, and Mr. Dallweather looked up with a start, "I do believe you've made the acquaintance of Mr. Dallweather?"

That gentleman shot to his feet and executed a deep bow.

"It was very kind of Mr. Dallweather to travel all this way," Brynnde went on as they seated themselves. She turned her head and gave a tiny cough that made Mr. Dallweather wince.

"Yes, well, of course," Mr. Dallweather stammered. "We've been neighbors for so long."

"Almost like family," said Brynnde. "You will have Mr.

and Mrs. Archambault for neighbors now," she went on. "Alas, it may be a while before they are ready for visitors. But I'm sure we will all meet again at the holidays, if my brother continues the tradition of the Christmas ball."

"Oh," said Mr. Dallweather, his brow creasing as the seed Brynnde planted met, if not fertile ground, enough good soil to begin to sprout. His gaze met Violet's, and Violet dropped her eyes shyly. "Oh," he said again, "I hadn't really thought…"

Violet lifted her head. "How are Ivy and Dane and…?"

Mr. Dallweather clapped his hands together, worries evaporating. "Very well! Just the other day…"

Brynnde stopped listening and allowed her attention to drift to the tall windows. There were clouds but no rain. She hoped the weather would stay dry just one more day. She didn't demand sun on her wedding day—it was November, after all—but if she could just stay dry for a change, she would be satisfied.

BUT THE SUN did come out the next morning, the clouds from the day before broken into high, white puffs that bore no threat. Molly dressed Brynnde in her cornflower blue dress, remarking, "It do look so nice with your eyes."

"And how are things with Geoffrey?" Brynnde asked.

Molly blushed. "Well'm, it's early days, but…"

"But?" Brynnde prompted. Her eyes met Molly's in the mirror as she allowed the maid to fix her hair.

Molly ducked her head. "But for now we'll just get you married and worry about me another day," she said roundly.

· · ·

A few hours later they returned to Ridgemow from church and went into the drawing room to wait for breakfast. "Happy?" Garrick asked.

Brynnde's gaze swept the room and found Violet who, yes, was seated in a corner with Mr. Dallweather. The two appeared to be in deep conversation and oblivious to the world around them.

And there was Tessa, like a ray of sunshine, bright and relaxed as she stood with her new siblings. When she forgot to wear her guarded, haughty expression, Tessa came across as quite charming.

Among the crowd around Tessa was the young Lady Elisabeth, Graeme's new wife, and Graeme beside her. All that trouble... But Brynnde could not nurse any resentment or grudge. It would be clear to a blind man that they were meant for one another and ridiculously contented. Even tall, long-faced Honora was smiling in the face of her younger sister's happiness.

Happiness! The word brought Garrick's question back to Brynnde and she looked up at him. He was still thinner and paler from the time spent at The Crowned Lion, but the bridal trip to Italy and Greece would change that and the warmer climate would be good for her, too. And the romantic atmosphere might help Molly and Geoffrey...

Garrick noticed her staring and cocked an eyebrow at her. "What are you planning this time?"

"Nothing," Brynnde said. She took his arm as they were called in to breakfast. "For now."

ABOUT THE AUTHOR

M holds a Master of Arts in Writing, Literature and Publishing and a Bachelor of Science in Radio-Television-Film. She has a love of Shakespeare, having both performed and taught his work, and also interned on Hollywood film sets. She then worked in publishing before deciding to write full time. M lives in Livermore, California with her family and cats.

For more information:
pepperwords.com
visitors@pepperwords.com

ALSO BY M PEPPER LANGLINAIS

Faebourne: A Regency Romance